MW01106980

Come Hell Or High Water
A Longview Romance – Book 2

By Nancy M Bell

Print ISBN 9781771455022

Published By

Books We Love, Ltd.
Calgary, Alberta
Canada

Dedication:

For Shelby, Gracie, Sydney, Livy, Autumn, Paige, and Brooke. Follow your dreams.

Acknowledgments:

I am indebted to the following people for their help. My beta reader and number one fan, Catherine Heer for her advice and comments. WPCA chuck wagon driver Jordie Fike for his help with all things to do with wagon racing. Any errors are mine. Special thanks to Dr. C.D. Bell, B.Sc, DVM, MVetSc, DACVS, for his help and information regarding all things veterinary in this work. Any errors in the translation from doctor speak to layperson are mine. This book is better for their involvement and I am most grateful to them.

For Jenny
Thanks for giving
Michelle & company
a voice
Nancy

Chapter One

"C'mon, Storm." Michelle Wilson waited for the three-legged dog to make her way toward the truck. The black dog loped along in her own peculiar gait, tongue lolling out of her mouth.

Doc's wife, Mary, followed her down the path. She waited while Michelle got the dog settled in the truck and then leaned against the fender. "I'm worried about Luke, Chelly. He won't slow down and he's wearing himself to the bone." She wasted no time in sharing her fears out of the hearing of her husband of forty years.

"Is he still not feeling well? I know Cale is taking as many calls as he can to spare Doc from going out at night." Michelle glanced toward the surgery attached to the house behind Mary. "You need to hog tie that man of yours, woman." She smiled and patted her friend's arm.

"I might as well try and rope the wind. You know what he's like, stubborn as a mule and twice as ornery if you push too hard."

"Do you want me to ask Cale to speak to him about taking it easier? That's why he agreed to take him on as a partner in the first place."

"In theory, it sounds good, but Luke just can't seem to step back. I'm afraid he's going to drop in the traces one day. I made him an appointment with Doc Lewen but the old fool keeps finding excuses not to go." Mary dabbed at her eyes with the corner of her apron.

"If you're really that concerned, I'll talk to Cale when he gets home later. He's got surgeries most of the day. Maybe we can finagle a way to get that locum vet who was here at Christmas to come in for a bit. Can't remember her name at the moment. Rodeo starts soon and you know how Doc loves to hang around the chutes with his buddies."

Mary brightened. "That might just work, you know. See what your Cale thinks about that. By the way, have you seen Rob lately?"

"Not hardly. That boy needs to keep his ass home with one he married and quit nosing around me. He dumped me, for crap's sake, and I'm so done with him. Now he wants what he can't have. You'd think he'd have his hands full with Kayla and those dressage horses of hers. Why do you ask?" Michelle frowned at the match making older woman.

"Kayla dropped in the other day to pick up some wormer and some of Luke's special liniment."

"And..." Michelle prompted.

"Well, it's just she was asking if you'd mentioned anything about Rob hanging around the old place. Sounds like he's been coming home pretty late, and sometimes not at all. What with rodeo about to start and her going down the road in a different direction with those fancy horses of hers, I imagine she's a mite worried."

"First off, it's not his 'old place' anymore, it's Cale's now and there's no reason for Rob to be hanging around. I haven't seen him at any rate, so you can tell Kayla to bark up another tree. I think that boy did me a good deed when he dumped me. I don't envy her trying to keep tabs on him. Lord knows I tried for enough years."

"You've got a good man in Cale Benjamin, Chelly. Don't do something stupid if Rob Chetwynd comes crawling back with his hat in his hand. He always could wrap you around his little finger."

Michelle opened the truck door and slid into the driver's seat. Depressing the clutch she started the engine. After rolling down the window she closed the door. "Mary, the chances of me taking up with Rob again are slim to none. I'm not the starry eyed idiot I was, and I see him for what he is. He's got that bad boy cowboy charm thing going on, but he's not in it for the long haul. I'm surprised that girl got him as far as the altar to tell you the truth. He must have been stinking drunk."

"How did that happen anyway? Why weren't you in Vegas with him, you two fightin' at the time?"

"As usual, George was away at the rigs and I couldn't get anyone to mind the stock while I went gallivanting off to the NFR. I had a hard enough time getting up to Edmonton for the CFR in November, remember? That was a royal waste of time as far as spending time with Rob was concerned anyway. He was off with his drinkin' buddies and running around most of the time. He was acting strange even then. I should have known something was up."

"You think he was cheatin' on you at Canadian Finals before the National Finals Rodeo in Vegas?"

"I didn't at the time. Just thought Rob was bein', well, Rob. If you know what I mean. Now, yeah, I think he was eating grass on both sides of the fence. That might even have been where he met Kayla for the first time, I've never asked her about it."

"Might be best to let sleeping dogs lie, Chelly," Mary advised.

"You're probably right. But, back to Doc. I promise I'll talk to Cale about seeing what he can do to get Doc to slow down some. I gotta go, Mary. You take care and call me if you need anything."

Mary stepped back from the truck and waved as Michelle pulled out of the gravel parking area behind the clinic. Storm squirmed to get comfortable and laid her head on Michelle's knee. She turned the truck south when she reversed onto the road. The parking lot of the hotel was full of big bikes when she passed, probably guys down from Calgary for a drink. She shook her head. The allure of straddling a noisy machine when you could be riding a horse escaped her.

"Road trip, Storm. Gotta go to High River and pick up some feed for the horses." Michelle turned left onto the old Coal Trail road that cut across country between the two towns. *What the hell is Rob up to now?*" The black dog sighed and closed her eyes. "I know, dog. It's none of my business and I should stay out of it." Storm opened one eye and yawned. Michelle reached to turn up the radio at the same time her cell phone rang. She punched the button on the hands-free even though it didn't identify the caller. If it was a marketing call she was in just the mood to rip a strip off them. "Hey."

"Chelly, hey, it's me," Rob Chetwynd's voice crackled over the connection.

"Rob? Why the hell are you calling me?"

"Chelly, I need help. Can you come pick me up?"

She glared at the Bluetooth for a moment and shook her head. "I'm halfway to High River, where are you, and for God's sake why didn't you call Kayla? You know, the girl you married?"

Rob mumbled something unintelligible.

"What did you say? Where are you? What have you done now?"

"I'm at the cop shop in Okotoks...I need a ride." His tone was self-pitying.

"Where's your truck? Look, I'm almost to High River. I gotta pick up some feed. Why can't Kayla go and get you?"

9

"She's mad at me…again."

"Probably with good cause, Rob. Can't you call your mom, then?"

"She's on Kayla's side, even though she's still pissed at me for dumping you like I did."

"Where's your truck?"

"It's impounded. I got caught in a check stop and—"

"Rob, for God's sake! How stupid are you? You could have killed someone…"

"I know, I know. Kay already read me the riot act and told me to walk home," he sounded aggrieved. "C'mon Chelly, you always used to bail me out. Just this one more time, for old time's sake?"

She debated for a moment, torn between common sense which said to let him rot where he was and her old ingrained habit of bailing him out whenever he got in over his head. "Fine. I'll come after I finish at the UFA." She broke the connection and slammed her palm on the wheel. *Damn idiot, driving drunk. He must have a million angels watching over him.* Michelle considered calling Kayla, but dismissed the idea. The last thing she needed was to hear her belly ache about what a dink her husband was. *Like I don't already know.* She pulled into the UFA and picked up the supplies in short order. Gritting her teeth she turned the truck north on Highway 2A toward Okotoks.

Chapter Two

Michelle pulled into the Tim's drive through on the south end of Okotoks and ordered a medium double-double and an extra-large black coffee along with two donut holes for Storm. The big dog wolfed them down and licked her chops. Michelle snugged the coffees into the cup holder and ruffled the dog's hair.

"I must be losing my mind helping the idiot out. Maybe I should let him walk home." She giggled at the thought. Signaling, she pulled out into traffic and drove straight to the RCMP station. Telling Storm to stay, she parked in the shade and left the window down a bit. Rob met her at the end of the sidewalk, just inside the glass doors.

"Chelly Belly! I knew you'd come!" Rob hugged her and planted a sloppy kiss on her cheek.

"God, Rob! You reek. Don't call me that stupid name anymore or you will be walking home. What rot gut have you been drinking?" She disengaged herself from his clutches and turned on her heel. Without waiting to see if he was following she stalked back to the pick-up and opened the door. Rob arrived at the passenger side as she slid into the driver seat.

"Dog, get your ass in the back. Go on, git," Rob demanded wrenching open the door.

"Storm, stay," Michelle ordered. "You get in the back, Rob. I can't stand the stink of you, and I like the dog's company better than yours."

"You're kidding, right?" Rob raised his eyebrows, stopping with his hand on the door.

"Nope, dead serious. Either get in the back, or start walking." She grinned at the incredulous expression on his face.

Grumbling under his breath he climbed into the back seat, stretched out and covered his face with his Stetson. Michelle had hardly left the parking lot before snores emanated from the rear of the cab. Storm huffed, turned around a couple of times and collapsed on the passenger seat with a sigh of contentment. Michelle turned up the radio to drown out the snores from the back seat and made good time as she headed back south.

She pulled into the Esso at the north end of Longview and parked. "Rob, wake up. Where do you want me to drop you?" The recumbent figure in the back mumbled and tried to roll over. "Rob!" She turned and smacked him until he whipped the hat off his face and sat up.

"Leave off, Chelly. I'm up. What do you want?" He rubbed his face and blinked at her with bleary eyes. "Where are we?"

"The Esso in town. Where do you want me to drop you?"

"Hell, I don't know. I sure don't want to go home and get my ear chewed off by Kayla."

"Your mom's, then?" Michelle put the truck in gear.

"Shit, no! She's just as bad. I'll come out to the ranch with you. I can crash in the old bunkhouse—"

"Not happening, cowboy. I'll drop you at the Twin Cities. You can figure it out from there."

"Chelly, Chelly, what's happened to you? Where's my sweet little buckle bunny?" He half-climbed into the front seat and attempted to kiss her.

"Sit down, you ass. I'm not your anything, and I was never your buckle bunny." She shoved him hard enough to knock him into the back seat again. Before he could mount another attack she gunned the engine and pulled onto the blacktop. It only took a minute to get to the south end of town where she stopped at the gravel entrance to the hotel. "Get out."

"Aw, c'mon, Chelly—"

"Get out, now," she ordered.

"I don't wanna." Rob crossed his arms over his chest. "Make me."

"Oh for the love of God…" Michelle got out and stomped around to the other side. Wrenching open the door, she grabbed Rob by the ear and hauled him out. He landed in a heap on the gravel. "I said, get out!"

"Not fair! You used Mom's old trick." He attempted to stagger to his feet.

Michelle shoved him back down, slammed the rear door, and strode back to the driver side and got in. Before he could scramble to his feet she punched the accelerator and spewed gravel as she left the lot. Storm, roused by the noise, sat up and peered out the back window.

"Don't worry about it, girl. Let's get home and start chores."

Passing the vet clinic she noticed Cale's truck was still parked out back. Hopefully, Doc was spending some time with Mary and not out running the roads doing farm calls. Ten minutes later she turned onto the ranch road. She passed by the lane to her childhood home. Stacey must be making out all right with George back on the rigs. Michelle hadn't gotten any panicked phone calls for help in the past week from the city girl her brother had taken up with at Christmas. What her brother saw in the woman was beyond Michelle. She might be shacked up with George, but Michelle was pretty sure the little blonde still had her sights set on Cale. *Just old friends, my ass.* If Cale believed that line of bull, she certainly didn't. The engine growled as it geared down for the steep incline into the coulee and up the far side, rounding the curve she drove through the gatepost proclaiming she was entering the Chetwynd Ranch. Cale really needed to get around to changing that. There just hadn't been time before the winter set in when he'd bought the place last fall.

It was kind of weird living with Cale in the house she thought she'd be living in with Rob after they were married. Life was really surprising sometimes. Who would have thought

Mrs. Chetwynd would sell the ranch. It was true Rob never showed much of an interest until after the sale was final, but he'd been on the rodeo road so much he was never home anyway. Mrs. Chetwynd didn't want to stay there alone after her husband died, and it was beyond her to manage the livestock and maintenance by herself. Something Rob didn't appear to have taken into consideration.

"Good for us though, right Storm?" Michelle smiled at the animal beside her. Storm woofed and put her paw up on the dash peering through the windshield. "Yes, we're home, mutt. Your crazy puppy will be needing to go for a pee." Michelle pulled up by the chicken coop, let Storm out, and released Crazy Puppy from the mudroom of the house. *I really need to figure out a better name for that hound.* She waited while the dogs did their business, taking the opportunity to check on the cows down in the lower pasture and the horses in the corrals by the barn. When the dogs were done, she let them into the mudroom and closed the door. It only took a few minutes to transfer the feed from the truck to the feed room in the barn. She threw the horses some hay before heading to the house. Although the weather had warmed in the last few weeks it was a dry spring and the prairie still held to its buckskin colour tinted with just a hint of new grass. If they didn't get some moisture soon she'd have to haul another round bale down to the lower fields in the coulee for the stock. The wind picked up as she crossed the yard sending dust devils spinning across the hard packed ground.

Knocking the dirt from her boots she jumped up the two steps to the porch and let herself into the mud room. Storm thumped her tail and stared at the door to the kitchen while Crazy Puppy spun in circles. Michelle removed her coat and boots and let them both into the warm kitchen. She glanced at the clock. Three o'clock. Cale wouldn't be home for at least a couple of hours, maybe more depending on the surgeries, and if there were any emergency calls. Crossing the kitchen she entered what had been the parlour at one time, Cale had turned it into an office. Humming under her breath she opened the laptop on the old oak desk. Leaving it to boot up and connect to the internet, she went back to the kitchen and filled dog's dishes. Once the dogs had eaten, Michelle put fresh water down. The youngster galloped around the room yelping at his mother. Storm pinned him down with her one front paw and proceeded to wash his face. Chuckling, Michelle started the coffee pot and stuck her head in the fridge to see what the possibilities were for supper. Leftovers, she decided. Gramma's hash looked good. Left over beef, some potatoes, and vegetables. No prep, she'd just start it when Cale got home. That taken care of, she went through to the office and called up the database for the ranch program.

Pawing through the papers scattered on the desk she found the needed data on the bred cows and set about entering it. She paused to turn on the lamp when the natural light faded. Glancing out the picture window she smiled at the golden orange sunset. Rising, Michelle stretched and wandered over to kneel on the big chair by the window. Resting her chin on her arms on the back of the chair she gazed at the ever changing spectacle in the western sky. Across the coulee, lights winked on in the Wilson homestead. It was still half hers, really. But George and his little blond were welcome to it for the moment. No way was she going to live under the same roof as Stacey, not when it was pretty clear the woman was still interested in Cale. Besides, it was nice living here with Cale, making new memories with him to chase out the old ones of her childhood infatuation with Rob Chetwynd. Not that all the memories were bad, of course. She had loved Rob's Gramma Harner, and Mrs. Chetwynd had always been kind to her, still was when it came to that.

She shook her head and stood up as the light faded from the sky and the first stars peeked out in the dark heavens. Looked like another clear night, might still get some frost. Good thing it was still too early to hurt the hay crop. A glance at the clock showed it was almost six o'clock. Cale must be held up with an emergency. Well, better him than Doc. A frown creased her forehead remembering Mary's worries of earlier. Doc wasn't that old—she stopped and considered while doing a quick calculation—it didn't seem possible. The old vet must be close to 70, he'd always seemed invincible and ageless. Although lately he hadn't looked well, getting a bit breathless when he talked sometimes, letting Cale do most of the surgeries. She bit her lip. Mary was right. Her old friend did need to go see Doc Lewen. She'd talk to Cale when he got home and see if he could convince the older man to see reason.

Picking up a sheaf of papers from the shelf over the desk, she closed the ranch program on the computer and opened Cale's invoicing program. Storm wandered in with her offspring and made herself comfortable on the thick rug by Michelle's feet. "Might as well make myself useful, eh dog?" Cale never seemed to have time to keep up with the paperwork.

Engrossed in the intricacies of the billing and posting payments Michelle cursed when Storm scrambled to her feet barking. The puppy added his shrill yelps to the flood of noise. The kitchen door shut with a bang, she pushed back the chair and got to her feet.

"Storm! Leave off, it's just Cale. Pipe down, both of you. I'm in the office, Cale," she called.

Footsteps sounded in the hall as she turned to save her work and shut the program. Finished she looked up and froze. "What the hell are you doing here?" she demanded.

"I saw the vet's truck over at your old place and figured you might be lonely." Rob leaned a hip against the door frame effectively blocking the exit.

"Well, you're wrong. Get out. Go home to your wife." Beside her Storm crouched belly to the floor and growled low in her throat.

"What, you gonna sic that tripod mutt on me?" Rob laughed and took a swig out of the flask he pulled from a back pocket.

"Storm, no." The dog quit growling but kept her lips peeled back from her teeth. The puppy yipped from the safety of his mother's side. "Have you quit drinking at all? How'd you get here anyway, the cops still have your truck?"

"Can't you shut that mutt up? Hurts my ears."

"The puppy is fine, which is more than I can say for you. Move out of the way and I'll make some coffee. You shouldn't be driving when you're pissed to the gills." She shoved at him to make room in the doorway. "You need to get out of here before Cale comes home."

Rob grabbed her arm and yanked her toward him. "I told you, he's over at your old place with that little blonde who's shacked up with your brother. I'm bettin' he won't be home for a while, if you know what I mean." He waggled his eyebrows at her.

"Let me go, you jackass. If Cale is over there it's because some animal needs tending. Nothing else."

"Ah, Chelly Belly, you always were a trusting soul. C'mon, let me keep you company, for old time's sake." Rob dipped his head and tried to kiss her, his lips sliding off her cheek when she turned her head. "Is that any way to treat your first love? A little messing around won't harm no one. I'm thinking that's what that Stacey girl had in mind when she called the office."

"I said, let me go," Michelle warned. Rob grinned down at her and slid his arm lower, grabbing her butt.

"You always did have a fine as—"

Michelle's knee crunched into his groin at the same time she whacked the side of his head with the heel of her hand. He let her go abruptly and slid down the wall. She stepped over him and headed to the kitchen. Storm followed by leaping over the prone figure, the puppy however, decided to gnaw on his boot before clawing his way over. Rob slouched against the door frame half supported by the wall. He kicked feebly at the puppy while clutching his abused anatomy and muttering curses between groans. She spared him a glance before pushing the kitchen door open and stepping through. Served him right, the ass. A thread of guilt worried its way through her anger. Maybe she shouldn't have hit him so hard...No dammit, he got what he deserved. Rob had no right to come marching in and assume his advances would be welcome.

Water splashed out of the glass carafe as she filled it at the tap. Anger and frustrated annoyance coursed through her, setting her hands to shaking. Mumbling curses, she slid the pot unto the hot plate, filled the coffee maker and flipped it on. She kept an ear cocked for sounds from the hall. Surely, he should be up by now. She hadn't hit him *that* hard. Damned if she'd go check on his well fare.

The coffee was ready when Rob limped into the kitchen. "That was unfair, woman. Takin' advantage of me when I was only giving you what you asked for. We'll never have us no babies if you keep that up." He slumped into a chair at the table and put his head in his hands.

Michelle slapped a mug of black coffee in front of him. "How drunk are you? I want nothing to do with you. I've told you to leave. And, no, we are never going to have babies. You're married, remember, and not to me, thank God."

"Aw now, Chelly darlin', that was a mistake you know? You were pestering me about having kids and all that other stuff—" He peered at her through bleary eyes.

"All that other stuff? Like you boinking every buckle bunny that came your way when I wasn't with you? Like putting off the wedding date again and again? The only mistake was me not figuring out what a dink you really are. Drink the coffee and get out."

"You're a hard woman, Chelly. You can't throw me out of my own home. You always wanted to play house with me before, remember?"

"It's not your house, jackass. I have no intention of playing house with you, as you so quaintly put it. I'm calling Kayla to come and get you."

"C'mon, darlin', don't be so hard to get along with. No need to call the wife, unless you've gotten way more adventurous…you into a threesome?"

"That's it, Rob. I'm done!" She grabbed the mug of steaming coffee and dumped it on him.

"Bitch!" He surged to his feet and tackled her. They landed in a heap on the floor, Rob on top. Michelle squirmed and bucked in an attempt to dislodge him. He caught her hands over her head with one large hand. "That's it, show me how much you want me. You never used to like it rough, I must say this is an improvement."

He lowered his head and ground his mouth over hers forcing her lips open and attempting to shove his tongue in her mouth. She bit his lower lip hard enough that she tasted blood. A gasp escaped her and annoyance turned to fear when he ripped her shirt open with his free hand in retaliation. Michelle cursed herself as the exhalation allowed Rob to get his tongue in her mouth. She stilled for a moment, maybe if she quit fighting he'd come to his senses. Instead he shoved her bra up and pawed at her breast, pinching hard enough to leave a mark when she thrashed in protest. Suddenly, he was gone and Michelle opened her eyes, gasping for breath.

"What the hell is going on here?" Cale held Rob by the collar, twisting the material tight enough to half strangle him. He glared down at her before dragging Rob out the door and throwing him down the steps. "Don't come back here. I'll call the RCMP and have you charged with trespass if you show up here again, is that clear?" Cale thundered.

Rob picked himself up as Michelle reached the door and peered out from behind Cale. "Don't be blamin' me 'cause you can't keep your woman satisfied. She made the running, I only obliged her. For old time's sake." Rob winked at Cale. "Quite the spitfire you've turned her into, she wasn't ever that wild when I had her."

Cale pulled out his cell phone and started dialing. "You have exactly two seconds to get in that truck and get out before I hit send," he threatened. "Michelle, get back in the house, and for God's sake cover yourself up. Let me deal with the Lothario."

She shrank back from the anger in his voice and rigid stance of his shoulders. The pieces of her shirt were pulled together over the remains of her bra. She stumbled back into the kitchen and collapsed into a chair at the table. Her hands shook so badly it was all she could do to tie the tails of her shirt together. Really, she should go and change, but her legs refused to hold her. Storm slunk into the room and pushed her head into Michelle's hand. Absently, she stroked the big head and then lifted the whining puppy into her lap when he bumped against her leg. She should call Kayla and warn about the state her husband was in. In that mood he was sure to show up and demand his marital rights from her. If Kayla didn't show him the flat side of a frying pan up the side of his head she was an idiot. Michelle wished she'd had one to hand a few moments ago.

Fumbling for the phone in her back pocket she managed to dial Kayla. She waited impatiently for the woman to answer. "Kayla, it's Michelle. Rob was just here and he's stinking drunk. If I were you I'd lock the door and not let him in, but that's up to you."

"Why was he out there? I haven't seen him last night, was he with you the whole time?" Kayla's voice rose to a shrill pitch.

"Not a chance. The idiot got a DUI and called me to come and pick him up at the cop shop in Okotoks. They impounded his truck—"

"What? The bastard was driving my truck. I'll kill him when I get my hands on him."

"You might want to wait until he's sober so he remembers it. Right now he's crazy drunk. I dropped him at the Twin Cities earlier and I have no idea how he got a truck to come out here. He was so pissed he seemed to forget he didn't live here anymore. Cale just sent him packing. Look I gotta go. Be careful, Kayla. Rob can be a mean drunk sometimes."

"You mind your own man and let me handle my husband. I'd appreciate it if you'd quit coming onto him. He's married to me, or have you forgotten?"

Michelle stared at the blank screen in disbelief. *Coming onto him? What load of crap is he feeding her?*

"So, Michelle. You want to explain to me what was going on here? I don't appreciate coming home to find you screwing around on the kitchen floor. If you're not happy here, just say so." His expression was carefully blank, only the rigidity of his body betrayed his anger.

"Are you kidding me? Screwing around? He was trying to rape me for God's sake!"

"So you say. I'm sorry, Michelle, but it's all over town how you're still hung up on him and not over getting dumped."

"That's not true! I am over that jackass. I told you I love you, isn't that enough?"

"Those are just words, Michelle. What am I supposed to think when I find you half-dressed rolling around on the floor?"

"You could try believing me! You're a fine one to talk anyway. Do you think I haven't heard about you and Stacey?"

"What about me and Stacey?" His voice was so low it scared Michelle more than if he'd yelled.

"Everybody is quick to tell me they saw the two of you having lunch at the Steakhouse and having coffee at the café. Even tonight, you were over there before you came home. It's almost nine o'clock, what was so important you couldn't come home?"

"One of the mares had trouble foaling, your brother lost a mare and foal tonight. That's what

I was doing. Stacey was upset and worried about telling George, so I stuck around until she got hold of him. As for the rest of it, Stacey and I are old friends, friends, that's all. I've told you that over and over—"

"And I've told you over and over, I'm over Rob Chetwynd. But you don't believe me."

"And you don't believe me. Maybe we've made a mistake, Michelle." Cale sounded weary all of a sudden. "I think it best if you sleep upstairs for now. If there's no trust, what the hell are we doing?"

"Cale," she began.

"Not now, Michelle. I can't, I'm too tired to think and I've got a full day tomorrow." He walked past her toward the hall door.

"Cale," her voice was small, "do you want the ring back, then?" Tears choked her throat.

He stopped as if she'd shot him. Without turning around he leaned a hand on the door frame. "No, Michelle. Just you think about what it is you really want and then you decide if you want to keep it or not. Then we'll talk about what I want."

He continued on out the door, and Storm, the traitor, went with him. The puppy trailing behind his mother stopped in the doorway and looked back at her over his shoulder before disappearing into the shadows of the hallway.

Chapter Three

Michelle turned over and thumped the pillow for what seemed like the millionth time. The sky was lightening outside, pale gray light spilling through the window panes. A quick check of her phone revealed it was almost 5 am. Spring on the prairies meant long hours of daylight as the seasonal clock wound its way toward the summer solstice.

Knowing that sleep wasn't an option, she got up and padded over to the window. Fresh tears came unbidden as she looked out over the sweep of land coming alive under the strengthening daylight. Across the deep slash of shadow that marked the coulee, the Wilson home place was still in darkness. Stacey must find it lonesome over there by herself with George away so much. It didn't seem to make sense the woman would stick around just to do chores and keep the place up while George was gone. Her brother was no big catch in Michelle's estimation. *No, she's staying there so she can be near Cale.* She twisted the diamond and gold ring on her finger, slipping it on and off. Returning it wasn't something she wanted to do at all. But was she being fair to Cale? Maybe he was right and she wasn't really over Rob, childhood sweetheart and first love, and all that clap trap. She rejected the idea as soon as it crossed her mind. Whatever lingering romantic feelings she might have had for Rob Chetwynd were gone. Running her hands up and down her arms, she shivered. The boy she grew up with had changed into someone she hardly knew or recognized.

Dressing quickly, she stole downstairs and started the coffee for Cale. Before any sounds came from the front bedroom she crept back upstairs. She wasn't ready to face him just yet. More tears blurred her vision when she re-entered the bedroom she'd camped out in last night. How could he think she encouraged Rob? Honestly, as far as she could see, she'd never given Cale any reason to distrust her. How was she supposed to control what people gossiped about, for heaven's sake? Longview was a small town and the extended ranching community that surrounded it was fairly close-knit. Like any small place, everyone knew everyone else's business and felt it their duty to comment on it.

Cale's footsteps sounded in the hall below and the click of Storm's nails told Michelle he was up and about. Her heart stuttered when the steps halted at the foot of the stairs. She let out the breath she'd been holding when he continued on to the kitchen. Unsure whether she was disappointed or relieved, Michelle jammed the pillows up against the headboard and made herself comfortable, knees drawn up to her chin. She waited while Cale took Storm and Crazy Puppy out to do their morning business. She grinned, they really had to come up with a better name for the little dog. Nobody seemed to want the mutt, so it looked like he'd be staying with his momma. Her grin faded. Wherever she went, the dogs were going too. Storm was hers.

The growl of Cale's truck leaving the yard pulled her from her reverie. Better call Mary before she got wind of this latest fiasco. The shrill of the phone had her jumping up and racing down the stairs. *How did that woman find out so fast? It's only 7:30 in the morning.* "Hey, Mary," she answered the land line without checking the caller ID.

"Michelle? It's Stacey…"

"Why are you whispering? I can hardly hear you."

"There's a weird guy asleep on the porch. He keeps waking up and banging on the door, yelling for you to open up. I'm scared. Can you come over right away?"

"You didn't let him in, did you?"

"Lord, no. Are you coming? Do you know who it is?"

"Best guess is it's Rob Chetwynd. Cale threw him out of here last night. Kayla must have locked him out of their place." The sound of Rob yelling and hammering on the door interrupted the conversation.

"Michelle, I'm scared. What should I do? Please come over, right now."

"Stacey, I'm not Rob's keeper. He's not my responsibility. Call the cops and tell them you've got an intruder. Don't open the door and don't let him know you're there. He might well decide George is out of town and the place is empty."

"You really think I should call the police?"

"Yes. Or you can try calling Kayla, but I'd go for the cops if I were you. That idiot caused enough trouble here last night he can fall in the river for all I care. Call the cops, Stacey." Michelle broke the connection. She stared at the phone for a moment and then dialled Kayla.

"'Lo?" the woman's muffled voice was barely audible.

"Kayla, Michelle here. Did Rob show up last night?"

"He's not here, why? What did he do now?" She sounded resigned and aggravated at the same time.

"Stacey just called. It sounds like he's passed out at my folks place and scaring the crap out of her. I told her to call the cops, but I thought I should let you know in case you wanted to go and collect him."

"I know he's a really old friend of yours and you know him better than me, but what did you ever see in him?"

Michelle laughed. "The same thing you did when you married him in such a hurry. Rob can be charming with that bad-boy-but-I'll-be-good-for-you act. All little boy puppy dog eyes when he wants something or he's in a good mood. Honestly, I never saw this other side of him until lately."

"I'm really beginning to think I made a huge mistake." Her voice broke a bit.

"He must have pretty strong feelings for you, Kayla. He married you, and he wants to have babies with you. Two things I couldn't ever get him to really commit to. If you really love him, don't give up on him, but read him the riot act and let him know this nonsense has to stop. That's my advice, for what it's worth. You coming to rescue him?"

"Not hardly. Let the cops haul him in and he can cool his heels in jail for a bit. I'm not going to be running to his rescue every time he does some bonehead thing. High time that boy grew up. Thanks for calling, Michelle. I do appreciate it."

"Good luck to you with the growing up bit. You're a better woman than me, Kayla. Bye."

She glanced out the kitchen window as red and blue flashing lights lit up the house across the coulee. At least Stacey had the sense to follow through and call them. There was still coffee in the pot so she poured a mug and sat at the table by the window. Thank God, Rob Chetwynd was no longer her problem. Although, he seemed to still be capable of causing trouble enough in her life. The diamond on her hand caught the light and she twisted the ring on her finger. When Cale got home tonight, she'd sit him down and make him listen. Make him understand he was the only one she wanted.

In the meantime, she should call Mary. The woman had a nose for trouble and she'd know the instant she saw Cale something was wrong. The sun was well and truly up now, barn swallows swooped under the porch eaves, and across the hay field the meadow larks' rippling song filled the morning. Damn, they hadn't even set the wedding date yet and things were falling apart. Shaking her head, Michelle punched in Mary's number and waited while it rang. She glanced at the clock, 8:30 am, the woman should be in the kitchen by now washing up the breakfast dishes.

"Good morning, Longview Veterinary Clinic," Mary's voice was distracted and a bit breathless.

Michelle checked the number she'd dialled. Nope, this should be the house line. "Mary? What's up? It's Michelle."

"Oh, Michelle. I'm sorry, I'm so frazzled this morning I don't know if I'm coming or going. Luke had a bad night and I just packed him off to Doc Lewen's. Oh, by the way, have you seen Rob? Carolyn is beside herself since Kayla called in tears, something about Rob and the police…"

"Rob Chetwynd can go straight to hell. That's what I'm calling about actually. He showed up here last night drunk as a skunk, full of himself and expecting me to 'show him some loving', to quote him directly."

"Oh dear, what did Cale say? Is that why that boy looks like a puppy who's been kicked? Couldn't get hardly a word out of him this morning."

"That's the problem. Cale wasn't home. He walked in on Rob and me wrestling on the floor—"

"Why were you wrestling with him? You didn't do something stupid did you, Munchkin?"

"You too, Mary? Damn! That's exactly what Cale thought, jumped to the conclusion that I encouraged Rob to tackle me and rip my clothes off."

"What?" Mary's voice rose incredulously. "You were naked? Oh my Lord, no wonder that poor boy is so miserable."

"No, we weren't naked, Mary. I told Rob to take off and he wouldn't take no for an answer. I nailed him in the family jewels and he took exception to it and tackled me. I tried to get him off, but he's bigger than me. He ripped my shirt open and shoved my bra up to my neck. He had his hands all over me and shoving his tongue down my throat when Cale pulled him off."

"Oh my, oh my. What happened? Did Cale beat the snot out of him?"

"No, he threw him out and told him to git. Then he read me the riot act, basically walked out on me and said I needed to decide what it was I wanted. Then, we'll talk about what he wants, apparently. I don't need to think about what I want, I know what I want. Cale. But he doesn't believe me, and he obviously doesn't trust me. To top it off, that blonde bimbo George is shacked up with still has her sights set on Cale. She's just using George as an excuse to stick around here." Michelle finally ran out of breath.

"Oh, honey. I'm so sorry. Of course you didn't encourage Rob. But I had to ask, you know. In the past you've forgiven him a lot of things, and you loved him for a very long time, those ties and habits are hard to break. I think that girl does love your brother, by the way."

"Whatever. I am so done with that idiot. I should have got Grampa's gun and shot his ass full of buckshot. I'm gonna talk to Cale as soon as he comes home and get him to understand it's him I want. All day yesterday I was thinking about a date for the wedding. Maybe right before Stampede when everyone's in town?"

"Maybe you should wait on that, Munchkin. Give things a chance to settle down. What about September when the poplars and cottonwoods are all gold?"

"Depending on what Cale says, it might be a moot point anyway." She hesitated. "I asked him if he wanted the ring back last night. He was furious with me."

Mary's sharp intake of breath came clearly over the connection. "What did he say?"

"Nothing really. That's when he said I needed to figure out what it was I really wanted and then we'd talk about what he wanted. Damn it, Mary. Rob tried to rape me! He would have if Cale hadn't come home. What's gotten into him, he was never like that before? At least not that I saw, anyway."

"Did you call the police and make a report? Maybe you should."

"I didn't even think about it last night I was so upset about Cale being mad at me. He made me sleep upstairs last night, like he couldn't even look at me! I just want the whole thing to go away and forget about it. Nothing happened, really. Other than Cale misunderstanding."

"Why was Carolyn going on about the police then? She was some upset that Kayla decided to let him cool his heels in jail for a while. I think she's going down to see if she can get him released."

"Kayla?"

"No, Carolyn. She's planning on giving Kayla a piece of her mind."

"Carolyn should leave him where he is. Her coddling him is part of the problem and the reason he acts like such an ass. I told Stacey to call the cops on him."

"Stacey, what's Stacey got to do with it?"

"After he left here, he went over to George's and passed out on the porch. He must have woken up at some point, because Stacey called me in a panic about a drunk man pounding on the door and yelling for me. She wanted me to come over and take care of it. I told her it was Rob and to call the cops. I'm done with bailing him out of trouble. That's how this whole shit show started."

"What do you mean, Michelle? It started before he showed up at Cale's?" Mary sounded confused.

"The idiot got picked up for a DUI and refused to call Kayla. He phoned me when I was on my way to High River to pick up feed, played on our long history and I was fool enough to fall for it. I went and picked him up at the cop shop in Okotoks. He wanted me to bring him here and I refused. I dropped him at the Twin Cities and told him to figure out how to get home from there. I have no idea how he got out here."

"Did you call Kayla? Didn't she go and get him?"

"I did call her. She was some pissed, seems he was driving her truck and got it impounded. She's even angrier this morning. Carolyn might get an earful of her own if she decides to call her up on the carpet."

"Oh, dear. My stars, what nonsense that boy gets up to. You did the right thing, I think."

"Let's hope Cale sees it that way." Michelle sighed and leaned her head on her hand.

"Do you want me to talk to him? Explain what happened?" Mary offered.

"God, no! Let me handle this, please. The last thing I want him to think is that I was belly aching to you and getting you to intervene on my behalf. I'm a big girl now, stay out of it, Mary. You can't fix everything. Now, tell me what happened with Doc? Is he okay?"

"Lordy, I don't know, Michelle. He had trouble breathing last night, coughing up a storm. But the stubborn old goat wouldn't hear of me taking him into Oilfields General in Black

Diamond or to High River either. I finally talked him into seeing Doc Lewen this morning."

"Shit, he must really be feeling bad if he's gone on his own. Do you want me to come in to town and help with anything at the clinic?"

"Would you? I'm so upset I can't seem to get anything done. Can you look and see if Cale still has the number for the girl who came in to cover at Christmas. Carol? Carla? The pretty red head girl."

"Carrie. Her name is Carrie. Hang on and I'll look on his desk."

"Just bring it with you if you can find it. I don't want to bother Cale, the clinic is crazy today and there's farm calls still to do. If you can man the reception desk so I can stay with Luke when he gets home, I'd really appreciate it." Mary sounded relieved.

"I'll be right there. I have to bring Storm and Crazy Puppy. Can they stay in the kitchen with you? Puppy will wreak havoc in the clinic if he gets the chance."

"Of course, just get here soon, please. I gotta go, there's the door again."

"I'm on the way, Mary," she said to the dead line.

Wasting no time, Michelle found the locum's number and loaded the dogs into the truck. She spared Stacey a thought as she roared past the end of the Wilson lane. Had to give the girl credit for sticking it out. Either she really was crazy enough to have fallen for George, or she was pretty determined to hang around and

37

get her claws into Cale. Dismissing that little problem for the moment, Michelle turned onto the blacktop and headed for town. Shortly, she parked behind the clinic and let the mutts out of the cab. Storm hopped up the path toward the kitchen door. Crazy Puppy bolted around like a wild thing smelling everything in sight and marking his territory. Two of his siblings were out next door in Harvey's yard and the puppies had a noisy reunion through the fence. Michelle collected him, tucking the wriggling body under her arm and joining Storm who waited impatiently by the door.

"Hey Mary, I'm here," she called as she let herself in, shut the door and set Crazy Puppy on his feet. There was no answer and the bit of coffee in the pot was burning dry. Michelle flipped the maker off, removed the scorched pot, and went in search of the older woman. She must be out at the reception desk. Poking her head through to the clinic attached to the main house she found Mary dealing with an invoice, her hands shaking so bad she could hardly type. "Here, let me do that, Mary. What's wrong? Is Doc okay?" She took Mary's place when she stood up and finished the open billing. "Come sit down and tell me what's wrong. You're scaring me." Michelle drew her over to the two chairs in the reception area and sat down beside her. "What is it?" She took Mary's hand in hers.

"It's Luke." Mary sniffed back a sob. "He went to Doc Lewen's this morning 'cause I nagged him and…"

"What, Mary? Is he alright?" Fear pooled in Michelle's stomach and her head spun. It had to be serious to get the older woman in such a state. "Where is Doc, Mary? I didn't see him in the house? Is he with Cale?"

Mary shook her head, tears spilling down her cheeks. "No, he's not in the house," she managed to choke out. "He's on his way to Calgary."

"You didn't let him drive all that way when he's not feeling well, did you? I would have taken him—"

"The ambulance took him…" Mary dissolved in tears. "Doc Lewen called just before you got here. He sent him up to Oilfields in Black Diamond and the ER doctor stabilized him and sent him up to Calgary."

"Stabilized? Stabilized what? How bad is it?" Michelle gripped her friend's hand tighter.

"It's his heart, Michelle. I knew something was wrong, I should have made him go sooner…"

"You know you couldn't make him do anything he wasn't ready to do. He must have been feeling really crappy to even go to Doc Lewen. Do you want me to take you up to Calgary right now? What hospital is he going to? Storm and Crazy Puppy can stay here, I'll let Cale know they're here and he'll take them home when he goes. They can go on calls with him if need be. The important thing is to get you up to Calgary so you can be with Doc and talk to his doctors."

"But, who's going to man the reception here if you come with me?" Mary wrung her hands, pulling free from Michelle's grip. "Luke would never forgive me if we left the practice unmanned."

Michelle thought fast. "Harvey's home, I saw the pups out in the yard. I'll go ask him to come over and hold down the fort. Any billing can wait til we get back, but Harvey will answer the phone and take care of any walk-ins." She got up and checked the appointment calendar. "Looks like there's no more appointments for today. Cale has surgery scheduled for another couple of hours and then some farm calls. Those can wait, it looks like, if need be. Does he know about Doc?"

"I haven't had a chance to tell him, he should be just about finished with the spay he's got on the table. Will you tell him, please? I need to go and get some things together for Luke, his slippers and, oh I don't know, other stuff." She got to her feet and hurried through the adjoining door into the house.

Michelle let herself into the back where the surgical suite, exam rooms, and kennels, were located. Cale was just coming out of surgery, leaving the tech to monitor the patient in recovery.

"What are you doing here at this time of day?" He removed the surgical mask, peeled off his gloves and tossed them both in the garbage bin. Stripping off his scrubs he deposited them in the laundry bin. "I don't have time to talk

40

right now, can this wait til later." Cale refused to look directly at her and busied himself with finding a pen to make notes on the animal's chart.

"Mary called. I have to take her up to Calgary." She hesitated.

"And you need me to know this because?" He glanced up at her.

"Doc's on his way to the hospital by ambulance…" Michelle fought back tears; her throat constricted so much she could hardly squeeze out the words. "He's had a heart attack, I think."

His head shot up and he met her gaze. Disbelief and worry etched lines in his face. "Damn! I told the old buzzard he should go get himself looked at last week. How bad is it?" Cale rubbed the back of his neck.

"I'm not sure. I don't think Mary knows, or if she does, she's not telling me."

"Are you okay to drive?" He frowned at her. "I can't leave here, there's surgeries scheduled…"

"No, I know. Doc would never forgive us if we deserted the practice 'cause he's sick. I'm gonna run next door and ask Harvey to come fill in on reception in case someone comes in, and he'll take care of the phones." She turned to leave. "Oh, I almost forgot. Storm and Crazy Puppy are in the kitchen. Can you take them home when you're done? Maybe take them with you on the farm calls? I don't want that puppy to wreck Mary's kitchen."

"Sure, I'll take care of them. I'll go over the farm calls, if there's nothing that can't wait till tomorrow, I'll reschedule them. Call me when you know something."

"Once I know something, you'll be the first one I call. See you later." Part of her wished Cale would offer some comfort, a hug, even a smile, but he was already prepping for the next procedure. She didn't have time to worry about that now, anyway. She beat it out the door and over to Harvey's.

Chapter Four

The drive to Calgary took forever in Michelle's estimation. She glanced over at Mary as they finally reached the southernmost end of the sprawling city. Thank God for the new extension that allowed her to bypass busy McLeod Trail and merge directly unto the Deerfoot higher up.

"He's gonna be fine, Mary. Doc's too stubborn to let a little thing like his heart get the better of him." She reached over and squeezed her friend's hand without taking her attention from the steady stream of traffic.

Tears glittered in the older woman's eyes when she lifted her head. "You're right, of course. He wouldn't dare leave me without so much as a good bye." A tremulous smile lifted the corners of her lips. "The old coot isn't ready to pack it in yet. Told me this morning he wasn't goin' anywhere for a long time. He's looking forward to bouncing your babies on his knee."

"Not sure when that's gonna happen, so he best be stickin' around for a long time."

"You're gonna have to work that out with Cale soon, you know. No sense letting things fester and get larger than they really are. You set him down and hash it out tonight when you get home, you hear me?" Mary wagged a forefinger at her.

She turned into the Foothills Medical Centre entrance. "We're here. I'll drop you at the emergency door and then I'll go find a place to park." Michelle stopped by the ER. Mary got out and hurried through the automatic sliding doors without a backward glance. Michelle edged back in the stream of vehicles and entered the lot in front of the Tom Baker Cancer Centre. As usual, parking was at a minimum, but she finally found a place to wedge the truck into in the far northeast corner of the upper level lot. She tossed the ticket with the time of arrival stamped on it onto the dash of the pickup and jumped down, pausing to lock the doors as she hurried across the pavement.

The waiting room was crowded but there was no sign of Mary. She must have talked her way to the front of the line and got taken in to see Doc already. Resigned to a long wait, Michelle found a place to sit and grabbed a tattered magazine. Fishing her phone out of her back pocket she sent Cale a text to let him know they were at the hospital. There was no return text, but he was probably still in surgery. At least, she hoped that was the reason.

Three hours, and four unsuccessful trips to the Triage desk to ask for information, later, Michelle wandered back to the waiting area. It was still as crowded as ever but she found an unoccupied bit of floor in the corner. She slid down the wall and kicked her feet out in front of her. Leaning her head back against the wall she closed her eyes. The events of the previous day, the tension with Cale and worry for Doc, caught up with her. Against her will, her eyes kept closing and she couldn't concentrate on the news cast on the TV mounted high in the opposite corner. Cale had to listen to her about Rob. Damn the jackass, he was the one who dumped her. So why now was he sniffing around again? He didn't want her, but he was damned if anyone else was going to have her either, she guessed. Typical cowboy logic. She snorted through her nose. Like Grampa used to say, the man wants the milk without having to pay for the cow. Michelle stifled a giggle. It was somewhat insulting to be compared to a cow, but the analogy was pretty accurate. "I should have kneed him harder in nuts," she muttered.

* * *

"Michelle, honey, wake up," Mary's voice intruded on her dreams.

"What?" Michelle shook her head and pulled her knees up. "Is Doc okay?"

"They're taking him up to the Cardiac Ward. Once he's settled we can go up and see him." Lines of worry and fatigue creased the older woman's face. Her shoulders hunched and tears on her cheeks reflected the overhead lights.

"What did they say? Is he going to be alright?" Michelle scrambled to her feet and put her arms around her friend. The woman muffled her sobs against Michelle's shoulder for a few moments.

"That's enough. I promised Luke I wouldn't cry. He's going to be fine." She smiled through the tears.

"What did they say?" Michelle persisted. "If he's going to the Cardiac Ward he must have had a heart attack. How bad is it?"

Mary wiped her eyes with the back of her hand. "Just a scare the doctor said. He's had a mild attack and with rest and the right medication he should be right as rain in a bit. They're going to admit him to keep an eye on him and to make sure he rests."

"What do you want to do? Are you going to stay in Calgary or do you want me to run you home?"

"Oh my Lord! What time is it? Those dogs are still shut in the kitchen, that puppy will have destroyed the place by now." Mary bit her bottom lip.

"Don't worry, Mary. I asked Cale to get them, he's gonna take them on the farm calls he can't reschedule and then take them home. Your kitchen should still be standing when you get back." Michelle grinned.

"Thank heavens for small mercies, I guess," Mary replied.

"Should I book you a hotel room? There should be something up in Motel Village by

46

McMahon Stadium." She referred to the cluster of hotels and restaurants near the football stadium up the hill to the east of the hospital. "There's bus service, or I have some cash on me you can use for a cab after visiting hours are over."

"I've got an old friend who lives close by. I'll call Emma and see if I can crash there. C'mon, let's get up there and see if we can get in to see that man of mine." Mary grabbed Michelle's hand and pulled her down the hall toward the main lobby and the public elevators.

The area was packed and they had to wait for two elevators before they could squeeze into one. Michelle trailed behind Mary as she marched off the elevator. Bypassing the nurse's desk she strode along the hall and turned in at a door near the end. Michelle paused in the door way and took a deep breath. The hospital smells invading her nostrils stirred up best forgotten memories of visiting her dad in his last illness. She took a steadying breath and closed her eyes. *Doc is not dying. Get over yourself and get in there.*

"Chelly, are you coming?" Mary stuck her head back out the door. "Oh, there you are. I thought I lost you for a moment."

"I'm right here. Hey, Doc. You'll do anything to get out of farm calls," she teased him while she hovered in the entrance.

"Get yer butt in here and give an old man a kiss," Doc's voice was thin and a bit reedy.

The clay colour of his face sent fissions of fear through Michelle, as did the quiver of his hands on the cover. Forcing a smile on her lips she crossed the tiled floor and planted a kiss on his cheek.

"Careful, young lady. My wife is a mighty jealous woman." He squeezed her hand and winked. "I'm fine, girl. You look like you're already on the way to my funeral."

"Don't even say that," Michelle gasped and glanced at Mary.

The older woman blinked and fished in her purse. "I've got to call Emma," she said waving a cell phone before she exited the room.

Doc's eyes followed her. "Oops, I'll have to apologize to her in a bit."

Michelle patted his hand. "Not something you should be joking about given the circumstances." She glanced around the room and waved at the closed privacy curtains around the bed.

He glowered at the monitors beeping and tracing squiggly lines across their screens. Doc plucked at the electrodes protruding from his hospital gown which apparently angered one of them as it emitted shrill alarms.

She slapped at his hand. "Now you've done it." Michelle moved out of the way as a herd of care givers arrived like the cavalry.

"Get away, I'm fine, I'm fine," Doc protested while they swarmed around him. One nurse escorted Michelle out of the room. She ran into Mary outside the door. The woman's face was paper white and she trembled so hard Michelle was afraid she'd fall.

"He's okay, Mary. The old goat yanked on those wire thingys they've got attached all over him. He's fine." Michelle gathered her friend into her arms.

"I'm gonna kill him, I swear. Just as soon as he's well enough." Mary laughed and cried at the same time. "I got a hold of Emma, she's on her way over. Promised to stay until I'm ready to leave Luke, and I can bunk at her place as long as I want."

"That's a blessing." Michelle glanced at the closed door. Doc's voice could be heard arguing about something but she couldn't make out the words. She glanced at Mary and grinned. "I'll stay til she gets here."

The commotion within died down and the door opened. "Hello, I'm Dr. Winston, the cardiologist in charge of Mr. Cassidy's care. He's been given a sedative to calm him and he should sleep for a while if you ladies would like to take a break. The prognosis is good if he'll just let us take care of him. Perhaps, you can have a word with him when he wakes up?" Dr. Winston eyed Mary.

"I'll certainly try, doctor. Thank you for your patience with him," Mary replied.

"Just doing my job." He smiled. "If you have any questions you can ask Mr. Cassidy's nurse, she'll be able to answer most inquiries." Dr. Winston hurried off, unclipping the beeping pager on his belt as he strode away.

"Look at the time," Mary consulted her watch, "you should get on the road, Chelly. It's getting dark and you've got chores to do still. The stock doesn't care if Luke is sick."

"I know, but I'll wait until Emma gets here. Did you tell her how to find us?"

"Here she is now," Mary exclaimed and rushed down the hall to embrace a tall woman with strong handsome features.

The two women walked toward Michelle, arms around each other's waist, heads close together. "Hi, Emma," Michelle greeted the newcomer. "I'm glad you could some so quick. I really need to get back to the ranch but I didn't want to leave Mary on her own. Thanks so much for coming." She hugged her.

"You should run along, Chelly. Cale will have finished at the clinic and the farm visits long ago. He'll be worried about Luke, and about you. Have you texted him with any news?" Mary clucked like a mother hen.

"Crap, no, I forgot with all the carry on in there." She tilted her head toward Doc's room. "I'll try to call him when I get out to the truck. Call me if you need me, Mary. Or, if he takes a turn…"

"Don't worry your head, Chelly. You heard the doctor, he just needs to rest and behave. You run along now."

Michelle poked her head in the door. Doc was asleep, snoring softly. He did look a bit better with more colour in his face. "Don't you dare die on me," she whispered so Mary couldn't hear. "I'm not ready to do without you, and you have to bounce my babies on your knee." She smiled and sniffed back a sob. Backing up and turning around, she hugged Mary and smiled. "Okay, I'm off then. Thanks again, Emma."

She left the hospital and paused at the entrance to the parking lot. Where did she park the damn truck? Somewhere...Michelle surveyed the multitude of vehicles in vain. Finally, she pulled out the keys and pressed the unlock button. From the far side of the lot a flash of lights beckoned her. Bother and damn, all the way to the farthest corner. A few minutes later she slid into the cab and called Cale. She tapped her fingers on the wheel while the phone rang and rang. Finally the answering service kicked in. *Humpff, maybe he just doesn't want to talk to me. But he must be anxious for news about Doc. Maybe he's still out doing farm calls.* She checked the time on her phone. Eight-thirty. *I sure as hell hope he hasn't left Storm and Crazy Puppy in Mary's kitchen all this time. I'd best stop there on the way home and make sure.* She fired off a quick text to Cale, saying she was just leaving Foothills and Doc was admitted so they could monitor his condition.

Her eyes burned and the oncoming headlights half blinded her. Maybe she'd talk to Cale tomorrow instead of tonight, she felt like death warmed over. The unintentional thought of death send a shudder through her. Instead, she turned her thoughts to the upcoming rodeos she needed to get to. Calgary was a no go this year, she missed qualifying by a few points. The points she was accumulating now would count toward qualifying for next year. She needed to be in the top six in her association. She'd been running well since Christmas and things were looking good. Currently, she stood atop the leader board. Last year was rough, losing Tags after the Canadian Finals Rodeo the year before had been a big blow. It had taken the whole season to work out the kinks with Spud. She grinned, who would have thought that a horse bred in P.E.I. would end up barrel racing in Alberta. The big chestnut gelding was flashy with lots of chrome, but as Grampa had often said, 'you don't ride the colour'. Once the gelding got over the nonsense of trying to buck her off every time she threw a leg over his back Spud had been unbeatable this year. It made up for the multitude of times she'd eaten dirt when the gelding would rather sunfish than turn a barrel.

Michelle turned off the number 2 highway and drove the short distance into town before she pulled into the clinic. No lights showed in the house and only the reception area light was on in the clinic. Cale's truck was nowhere in sight. Sighing, she got out of the pickup and picked her way up the back walk in the dark. No barking heralded her approach which was a very good sign. The last thing she felt like doing was cleaning up Crazy Puppy's mess all over the kitchen. Extracting the key from its hiding place she opened the back door. Except for a dirty coffee mug on the counter, the place was clean and tidy. Thank God. She paused for a moment and looked around the familiar room. "Get better quick, Doc. We need you here," she whispered.

Shaking her head, she left the house and locked the door. A brief stop at Harvey's to thank him for covering the reception desk and update him on Doc's condition slowed her down a bit. The moon was riding high in the sable sky when she passed the Wilson lane and continued on to Cale's, and home. The light from the kitchen window illuminated the yard. She parked in the lee of the building. Cale's truck was missing so she poked her head into the house to check on Storm and her offspring. The two dogs were curled up on the large dog bed by the wood stove. She ducked back out without waking them and headed to the barn to start chores. Spud was in the barn, along with a young horse she was bringing along for next year. She'd taken Rain to a few smaller events and the mare had done rather well for herself. She didn't have the explosive speed of the chestnut, but she was smart and cat like on her feet. The time they lost in the straight away she more than made up for with her turns, especially on the top barrel. She hummed as she tossed hay in to them and readied their grain. Flipping the light off she went to do the chickens.

The wind whipped up the coulee and dust devils swirled across the yard. Michelle shivered and pulled the collar of her coat up around her ears. Just because it was mid-April didn't mean it couldn't turn bone chilling cold. The chicken house was warm inside, the hens all settled in their roosts. She gently removed the eggs from under them and placed them in the basket she kept on a shelf. "Thanks, ladies," she told them. Carefully, she closed and latched the door, shoving an old burlap grain sack under the bottom of the door to stop the draft. The cold hurried her on her way to the house.

After shedding her outer clothes in the mud room, Michelle started a pot of coffee and then washed the eggs in the sink. Placing them in a clean carton she stored them in the small fridge kept for that purpose. There was no message on the house phone and no answer to her text when she checked her cell phone. "Cale, where are you?" It was almost nine-thirty. Surely, he couldn't still be doing farm calls? Against her will, she looked toward the Wilson place across the coulee. The large yard light was on and as far as she could make out, only Stacey's fancy low slung car was visible. "Hmmpf, so where are you?"

The coffee maker beeped and she poured a huge mug. Taking it with her, she went into the office and spent an hour entering data. Closing the program and shutting down the computer, she stretched and yawned. The coffee hadn't done much to curb her exhaustion. Rubbing her eyes, she took the mug to the kitchen and let Storm and Crazy Puppy out to do their business.

Shivering in the doorway, she watched them casting about for a good place to relieve themselves. "Hurry up, dogs, I'm freezing," she called. A few clouds scudded across the moon and she glanced up. No headlights traced out the road around the coulee. Jealousy stabbed suddenly. Maybe Stacey wasn't home after all, maybe she was out with Cale in his truck. She twisted the diamond ring on her finger, started to yank it off and then changed her mind. *Nope, I'm not cutting and running. I'm sure about what I want. I only hope Cale hasn't changed his mind.* Her teeth gnawed her bottom lip. Storm and Crazy Puppy trooped back inside and she shut the door.

Michelle turned out the kitchen light and went down the hall, Storm and Puppy following. Storm turned into Cale's bedroom and flopped on the mat by the bed. The puppy snuggled with her. She hesitated and glanced up the stairs toward the room she'd occupied the previous night. Until Cale cooled off maybe she should just stay up there. Her heart said otherwise, though. It would be harder for him to ignore her if she was in his bed. Making her decision, she joined the dogs and flicked off the hall light. The wind whistled through the cracks around the windows. They really did need to get around to replacing the windows this summer. Stripping to her skin, she slid into the bed and stared at the ceiling. Eventually, she turned off the bedside lamp and quit checking her phone for the time, or a text from Cale. Despair knotted in her chest and soured her stomach. Was this how it ended? Before it really began? And all because Rob was a jackass and thought he was God's gift to women. She ground her teeth and pounded the pillow.

Her nose prickled with the pressure of unshed tears and her tired eyes burned. Finally, she gave into the tears and let them come. Storm got up and licked her face which only made her cry harder. The black dog heaved herself onto the bed and pushed her head against Michelle's shoulder. "Oh, Storm, what are we going to do if he decides he doesn't want us anymore?"

Outside the wind picked up and rain rattled the window panes. She shivered and pulled the duvet higher around her ears. Storm whined and shifted so Michelle tugged the blankets from under her and took the dog under the covers. Crazy Puppy circled a few times and then jumped up onto the end of the bed.

Chapter Five

The thump of Storm jumping off the bed woke Michelle. She rolled over and peered at the clock radio through half-open eyes. God, it was six-thirty and the sky was grey. Struggling to a sitting position she surveyed the room. Cale's side of the bed was empty, the pillow showing no indent where his head had laid. Despair and fear washed over her in a cold wave. He didn't come home last night. What was that supposed to mean, and how was she supposed to react to that?

Storm whined and Crazy Puppy licked her bare leg where it dangled over the edge of the bed. "Okay, okay, I'm coming. Keep your hair on, dog." Dressing in haste she padded down the hall with the mutts in hot pursuit. Frost glittered on the frozen earth and dressed everything in lacey ice crystals. Michelle hovered in the doorway while the dogs went about their business. Her breath hung in the air and she shivered; the boards of the mudroom floor cold on her bare feet. "C'mon you guys, in," she commanded and Storm obediently came as fast as her three legs would take her. Crazy Puppy galloped behind abandoning his exploration of the fence posts in the corral.

She dumped food in the dog dishes and filled the water bowls. Hurrying down the chilly hall to the bedroom, she dressed and returned to the kitchen. Grabbing a go mug of coffee and a breakfast bar she bundled up and made her way to the barn. The truck needed to go into Harry's today for a tune up and she might as well drag the trailer in as well and get it a once over. Later, she was scheduled to do some practice runs at Prairie Winds. Pat was training for the Kananaskis rodeo in Coleman as well as Michelle. With any luck there wouldn't be a big snow storm to drive through. Ever since the accident that took Tags, Michelle hated to haul in the snow. But if she wanted to rack up enough points to get to the CFR and finish high enough in the standings at the end of the year to qualify for Calgary, she'd best bite the bullet and get it done.

She brushed Spud and Rain while they ate their grain and then threw them hay. Spud's blanket had come askew and she straightened it before leaving to check on the outside stock and do the chickens. Once assured everything was in order, Michelle ducked into the house to check on the dogs and grab the truck keys. "You two be good, you hear," she told the dogs. Crazy Puppy looked up and woofed. "You, especially. No chewing my chair pads, you hear?"

Making sure the inner door and the mudroom door were shut properly, she climbed into her pick up and waited for the glow plug before starting the engine. The throaty roar of the big diesel sounded extra loud in the morning stillness. A flock of magpies chastised her from the ridge of the barn roof. She giggled, since they were members of the Corvidae family, maybe they were a murder, or a parliament, of magpies rather than a flock. Who knew? Michelle shrugged. While waiting for the truck to warm up she checked her phone—no message from Mary, and no word from Cale. In Mary's case, no news was good news, she supposed. However, Cale's silence weighed on her heart.

"God damn Rob to hell and back, and I should have my head read for agreeing to go pick the jackass up in the first place. Old habits die hard, I guess. But I am so done with him." She ground her teeth with frustration. *Should I call Cale? But do I really want to know if he's with Stacey?* She glared across the coulee at the ranch she grew up on. "Which one of them will I kill first...Stacey or Cale?" she muttered. With the ease of long practice she put the truck in gear and hooked the big gooseneck trailer. After one last look at the house across the coulee she pulled out onto the gravel road and headed for town. Stacey, she decided, I'll kill her first.

She stopped at the clinic and ran next door to ask Harvey to watch the reception desk again. Cale would have to get a temp to cover while Mary was in Calgary. Taking a short cut she dashed across the back yard and vaulted the low fence. She stopped in her tracks at the sight of Cale's pick up behind the clinic. Without thinking, she keyed the code in the door lock on the rear door and let herself in.

"Cale? You here?" Only the sharp yip of one of the patients answered her. She continued along the hall past the exam rooms. "Cale?"

"Michelle? Is that you?"

She followed his voice toward a small office at the end of the hall. Cale emerged from the door blinking sleep from his eyes.

"What time is it? Have you heard how Doc is?" He scrubbed both hands over his face and shoved the wayward shock of hair off his forehead.

"It's about eight in the morning. I haven't talked to Mary since last night, but Doc was stable and being his cantankerous self when I left the hospital." She hesitated and then looked up at him. "Why didn't you come home last night?"

"I was out late on calls and then I needed to come back to the clinic to restock some stuff and drop off some specimens to go to the lab. Honestly, Michelle, I wasn't sure there was anything to come home for." Cale regarded her intently.

"What's that supposed to mean? I had your dinner in the oven and I waited up for you."

"With Rob for company? Kayla called my cell wanting to know if I knew where he was. She figured you might know." He brushed by her and flipped the switch on the coffee machine in the waiting room.

Michelle took a deep breath and fought to control the anger surging through her. It was a valiant effort but doomed to failure. Really, she wasn't sure why she even tried. "You know what, Cale? Screw you! If that's what you want to believe then there's nothing I can do about it. Maybe Kayla should put a GPS on her husband. He's not my problem anymore." She stomped by him toward the rear entrance. In the door way she swung around. "I'll be out of your way soon, so you can go home without worrying about running into me. Once Harry is done with the truck and trailer I'll be going down the road. Rodeo starts next week and I'm gonna camp out at Pat's until then. Save trailering over there every day, and I won't be taking up space in your house." Head held high she shoved the door open. "Oh, by the way, Harvey says he'll cover the reception until you can get a temp. Don't bother to thank me."

"Michelle, I didn't mean it like that."

"The hell you didn't." She slammed the door behind her. Childish, she knew, but it helped to relieve some of the anger thrumming through her. Harvey was crossing the yard as she drove out of the parking lot, she waved but didn't stop. Harry's was just down the main drag on a side street. She parked out front and let herself in.

"Hey, Harry. How's it hangin'?" she greeted him.

"Mornin' Michelle. Good, how about you?"

"Been better, Harry. Did you hear about Doc?"

"Grape vine's workin' fine." He grinned. "Heard the ambulance took him up to Calgary. Any news this mornin'?"

"Not yet, but if anything was wrong Mary would have let me know. The rig's parked out front, how long do you think it'll be?"

"Few hours, sorry. I had an emergency road call and I'm behind. You wanta wait at the clinic and I'll call you there. Or not," he added at the sour look on her face.

"You got something I can borrow? If it's gonna be that long I'd like to run up to the hospital and see Doc. Take Mary some clothes and stuff?"

"Sure, just don't be gone all day." Harry tossed her his own truck keys.

"Thanks, man. I won't be more than three or four hours. They're keeping visitors to a minimum still. But I'll feel better if I actually see him, you know?"

"Skedaddle, Chelly. The rig'll be ready by the time you get back. Give Mary my love and tell that old buzzard he'd better get well quick. He owes me from the last poker game."

"I'll do that," she flung the words over her shoulder as she sprinted to the old red Chevy.

* * *

Michelle hesitated outside the door to Doc's hospital room. Taking a deep breath to

62

calm the quivers in her gut, she steeled herself for the worst and pushed open the partly closed door. Mary sat in a chair holding her husband's hand. She raised a finger to her lips and nodded toward the sleeping man in the bed. Extracting her hand, she rose quietly and hugged Michelle before leading her back out into the hall.

"How is he?"

"Luke's much better today. The doctor was in and he seems pleased with the progress. They figure to keep him another couple of days to be sure he's out of the woods and the medication is working. Then I can bring him home."

"That's great news, Mary." Michelle hugged her friend.

"Have you talked to Cale about calling the locum? Luke is going to have to take it easy from here on, even if I have to hogtie the old man to a chair." Mary grinned.

"I talked to Cale, but I didn't get a chance to mention the locum," Michelle didn't want to worry Mary with her problems.

"Like that is it? Well, you'll have to work it out, living in the same house and all." She patted Michelle's arm.

"Sure, that'll happen," she said sceptically.

"What?" Mary demanded, albeit sotto voce. "Spit it out, girl."

Michelle glanced at the man in the bed and nodded toward the door. Mary eased her hand out of her husband's and got to her feet. They slipped out of the room and into the hall.

"I know you hate to leave him, but I don't want to wake him up, either." Michelle pulled the door almost shut, leaving it a tiny bit ajar so they could hear if Doc needed something. "Rodeo starts in a week, I'm entered at Coleman and…well…I'll be gone a fair bit…"

"And? What aren't you telling me? Did that foolish boy kick you out over Rob's stupidity?"

"Not exactly," she prevaricated. "I'm taking Spud and Rain, and probably the dogs, and staying at Pat's over at Prairie Winds. I need to practice every day anyway, and Rain needs to learn the pattern—"

"You could still go home at night, I'm sure Pat has a couple of stalls you can rent." She fixed her young friend with a gimlet eye.

"Yeah, well…I'm staying in the trailer. It's got heat and a little kitchen. I'll be fine. I don't think Cale wants me around right now. It's like he can't bear to look at me." She sniffed. "Damn, hospitals always make my nose run."

"Ummhmm, the hospital, that's it." Mary handed her a tissue.

"Look, you've got more to worry about than my love life, or lack thereof. Concentrate on getting that man home and healthy. I can manage for a while without your matchmaking." Michelle managed a watery grin.

"I spoke with Carolyn last night for a bit," Mary began.

"Not about me, I hope," Michelle cut in.

"More about Rob and Kayla, and a bit about you. She's worried sick about the boy, he

64

seems hell bent on self-destruction. I guess Kayla was at Carolyn's place in tears over him not coming home and passing out in the parking lot of the Twin Cities. One of his buddies dumped him on their doorstep and Kayla had a devil of a time getting him inside. Carolyn is worried the girl is gonna give up on him and pack it in."

"Maybe she should," Michelle replied. "He's changed, Rob never used to be mean, not even when he was drunk. A pig sometimes, and stupid, but not mean. He didn't want me when he had me, now I've told him where to go and how to get there, he's obsessed with me. Kayla should cut her losses and get out while she still can."

"That's hard, Chelly."

"Yeah, well, he isn't content with screwing up his own life up, now he's screwing with mine too."

"I called Dolores last night too." Mary glanced at her out of the corner of her eye.

Michelle covered her face with her hands. "Not Cale's gramma! Damn, Mary, do Peggy and Carson know too? His parents will think I'm the whore of Babylon, for God's sake. What with them walking in on me and Cale at New Years, and now Cale finding me flat on my back with Rob's hands everywhere they shouldn't be..."

"Did that boy hurt you?" Mary frowned. "I don't think Carolyn knows it went that far, or Kayla for that matter."

"He was trying, that's for sure. He figured when I wouldn't give him what he used to take for granted, he'd just take it. Any way he could. If Cale hadn't come home I'm not sure I could have got away from him. He was so pissed he was only thinking with the head under his belt buckle."

"Dear me, that does put things in a different light." Mary stroked her chin.

"What about Dolores? What did she say about Cale and me?"

"Only that the boy was some upset about something that had to do with you and Rob. I told her I thought there'd been some sort of misunderstanding but I didn't know the whole story," Mary replied.

"And she bought that? From Mary the Queen of the Gossips?" Michelle teased her.

"Mind your tongue, missy. Or I'll have to start making up some juicy nonsense to punish you." Mary smiled. "Seriously though, Peggy is worried about Cale. She asked Dolores to find out what she could, the woman wants to talk to you about whatever is wrong, but she doesn't want to stick her nose in where it's not wanted either."

"Do you think I should call her? I don't know what to do. Cale is so determined to believe the worst. Rather than keep fighting with him, I thought maybe the best thing I could do was just clear out for a bit."

"You think going out on the rodeo road is the best thing to do? He'll know Rob is out there too, probably at a lot of the same events." Mary worried her bottom lip with her teeth.

"If I want to qualify for the big shows I have to accumulate enough points, and money, of course. I'm not gonna let Rob dictate what rodeos I go to and what ones I don't. I won't have to see him, except maybe at some of the smaller ones. I'll just stay clear of the chutes and mind my own business."

"That's for you to decide. Cale is a good man, Chelly. Try to work it out before you leave if you can."

"Mary!" Doc's querulous voice came through the partially open door.

"Coming, Luke. Look who's here," she answered pulling Michelle into the room with her.

"Hey, vet man. What's the deal with skipping work?" Michelle leaned over carefully to hug him.

"Man's gotta do what a man's gotta do." He shrugged and grinned. "Mary conned me into goin' to see Doc Lewen, and before you can say Bob's your uncle, I'm hogtied in that tin can on wheels and hooked up to all kinds of contraptions. Not my fault. I'm ready to blow this popsicle stand."

"You'll stay put, until the doctors say you can go, you hear?"

"Yes, dear," he said meekly and winked at Michelle.

"You already for Coleman next week, Chelly?"

67

"Almost, I'm taking Spud and Rain over to Prairie Winds for the week and then leave from there."

"Rolly was in this morning, sweet talked his way past the nurses before visiting hours," Doc reported.

"What did that scallywag want?" Mary demanded. "He had no business tiring you out."

"Lord, woman! All I do is sleep, did my soul good to see the boy."

"Rolly going down to Coleman?" Michelle asked.

"Yup, he was askin' if I knew anyone looking to outride for him. One of his regular guys done broke his wing when they was practicing. You know anyone?"

"Is he paying?" Michelle did a quick mental calculation.

"I suppose he's paying the going rate. Why?" Doc's brow furrowed and his expression became wary.

"Nothin', I was just thinking—"

"You were just thinking nothing, young lady," Doc thundered. "Outriding is no place for a girl."

"Calm down, Luke. I'm sure Michelle has no intention of outriding for Rolly." Mary laid a soothing hand on her husband's arm and shot Michelle a warning look.

"I ride as well as any of them, and you well know it, Doc. But, no, I'm not thinking of riding for him." Michelle crossed her fingers behind her back.

"Well, good then, that's settled."

"I gotta go, Doc. I borrowed Harry's Chevy while he's going over the rig and I promised I'd have it back to him soon." She hugged the old vet and kissed his cheek. "You behave yourself, you hear."

"Take your own advice, Chelly Belly."

"Point taken." She grinned. "I'll see you before Coleman for sure. Take care, vet man."

Mary followed her out of the room. "Be sure to speak to Cale about the locum when you get back, and see if Mabel's daughter can look after the reception. Harvey's a dear soul, but we can't expect him to cover for me indefinitely."

"I'll do that first thing I get back," she promised. "Mabel's daughter is good idea, of if she can't do it, maybe Harvey's granddaughter can fill in."

"Thanks, Michelle. Let me know as soon as you've got it worked out. It will take a load off my mind, and Luke's too. Dive safe, love you, honey." Mary enveloped her in a huge hug.

"I'll call as soon as I know. If I can't reach you, I'll leave a message at Emma's." She extricated herself Mary and waved as she set off down the hall. She glanced back before she turned the corner for the elevator but Mary was already back at Doc's side.

Chapter Six

Michelle tossed the keys to Harry when he poked his head out of the shop at the back as she came through the door. "Thanks for the truck. Doc's doing good. I feel so much better for seeing him."

Harry caught the keys in mid-air and pocketed them in one motion. "Your rig's all set. I checked the pressure in the tires and added some air to the trailer ones. Changed your oil and filters, checked all the fluids. You're good to go. I got the invoice right here." He waved a yellow paper at her.

"How much do I owe you, you bandit?" Michelle leaned on the counter and pulled her wallet out of her back pocket.

"You wound me!" The mechanic held his grease stained hand over his heart.

"Sure, sure. What's the damage?" She laughed with him.

In short order she paid the bill and took the keys from Harry. "It's out back. You know where I usually park it."

"Thanks, Harry. You goin' down to Coleman?"

"Too busy, I gotta wait until High River for my rodeo fix, I'm afraid."

"See you then," Michelle said over her shoulder. Long strides took her across the puddle riddled lot and down the narrow alley to the back of the building. The lot opened up onto the laneway that ran parallel to Morrison behind the business that fronted on the main drag. Thank God, Doc was going to be okay. Losing him right now was more than she could handle, and Mary...Lord, what would Mary do if anything happened to Doc? Michelle shook her head and unlocked the cab. In moments she pulled out of the lot and headed for home. As she passed the clinic she pulled over and hopped out. Poor Harvey would need a break right about now, she figured.

"Hey, Harvey, how's it going?" Michelle's words trailed off and she stopped dead in her tracks. "Where's Harvey?" she demanded.

"He had some stuff he needed to take care of," Stacey shuffled some papers on the desk.

"Why are you here?" Michelle couldn't keep the frustration out of her voice.

"I was in town and stopped to pick up some stuff for George's mare and found Cale up to his ass in alligators. I offered to help out for a bit. That's all." Stacey met Michelle's gaze and raised her eyebrows, daring her to find fault with her actions.

"I'm sure he was thrilled at your offer." She scowled and turned on her heel.

"Did you need something? You came in for something," Stacey called after her.

She paused with her hand on the door and pivoted. "I thought I'd give Harvey a break and maybe see if Cale wanted a coffee, but I see you have that well in hand. No need for me to bother him." She glanced at the tray of take-out coffee sitting on Stacey's desk.

"He's in surgery, but it should be done in a few minutes. Do you want to wait and talk to him?"

Stacey's blue eyes were big and wide and Michelle resisted the urge to slap her. *Just happened to stop by, my ass. I wonder how George is gonna feel when he comes home and finds out she's been stalking Cale the whole time he's been gone?* "Nope, if he wants to talk to me he knows where I am." Even though part of her wanted nothing more than to see Cale and talk this mess out, the other contrary part that wanted to protect her from breaking her heart again urged her to get the hell out of there. The contrary part won and she wrenched the door open and left. As it swung shut behind her Cale's voice drifted out into the lot.

"Was that Michelle?"

She quickened her steps, suddenly only wanting to run as far away as she could. Michelle stepped up into the cab and pretended not to see Cale coming out of the clinic and down the walk toward her. Slipping the truck into gear, she pulled away. Once on the hard top and headed to Pat's, she allowed herself the luxury of wiping away the tears from her face.

"That was stupid," she chastised herself. "What the hell is wrong with me? I want to see him and then when he shows up I panic and run. Damn, damn, damn." She blinked in surprise when the Wilson Ranch sign appeared on her right. *Shit, how did I get here so fast? The angels must have been driving 'cause I don't remember anything after leaving Doc's.* Continuing on past the place where she grew up, she geared down for steep incline where the road dipped into the coulee and then climbed out again. The road ended at Cale's and she drove under the overhanging sign that proclaimed that this was the Chetwynd Ranch. Gritting her teeth, Michelle wished for the thousandth time Cale would get around to changing the damn thing. But then again, maybe it wasn't any of her business anymore. She glanced across the coulee where the familiar house and outbuildings squatted on the edge. She *could* always go home, it was still half hers. Pride made her reject that idea as soon as it surfaced. Maybe, just maybe, if Stacey was gone…and if George quit acting like king shit every time he came home. *Fuck, I'd have to be pretty desperate.*

The sun was fully up by the time she parked by the barn. In short order she transferred her belongings from the tack room and into the compartment of the trailer especially designed for that. Saddles, feed buckets, water pails, blankets and her tack box, along with mucking out utensils filled the area. Bags of feed went into the front of the trailer along with as many hay bales as would fit. The dividing gate of the three horse angle haul shut with a metallic clang. Michelle dusted off her hands and debated on whether to load the horses now or go get her stuff from the house first.

A gust of wind snatched at her coat when she stepped out of the shelter of the trailer. Crossing to the barn, she checked on Spud and Rain, they still had their heads in their grain buckets so she left them and went to the house. Storm and Crazy Puppy greeted her with enthusiasm. "C'mon, you two. I'm sure you want to go out." She opened the door to the mudroom and let them out into the yard. Keeping an eye on them through the wide kitchen window Michelle gathered up some food and a case of water. Anything else she'd just buy as the need came up. After carting the lot out to the living quarters of the trailer and stowing them away, she whistled for the dogs. They followed her inside and she shut the mudroom door and then the inner kitchen door behind them. Storm padded along with her when Michelle ventured down the hall towards the front of the house. The door to Cale's room stood open, she hesitated in the doorway and bit her lip. It shouldn't hurt that much, but it did. There was something almost final about removing her clothes from his room.

"Just get on with it," she muttered. Everything she needed fit into the large canvas carryall she pulled from under the bed. Finished in the bedroom, Michelle hefted the bag's straps over her shoulder and turned to leave. She paused in the door and turned back for one last look. *It's not like I'm leaving forever. We'll work this out, somehow. I know we will.* She hated the perverse nagging voice that reared its head. *What about Stacey? What if he decides I'm not worth the trouble?* Maybe leaving was a mistake, but how could she stick around when Cale didn't trust her? How could he actually believe she'd encouraged Rob or invited him into the house in the first place? Love without trust isn't love, at least that's what Gramma used to say. "Son of a bitch!" A flash of intuition flared in her head. "Maybe that's why I kept trusting Rob, even though my common sense said I should open my eyes. If I thought I loved him, then I had to trust him as well. What an idiot I was. Well, that's water under the bridge now."

It didn't take much time to collect her things from the bathroom. Her fingers lingered over the jar holding the toothbrushes before plucking hers out. In the doorway, Storm's head flew up and Crazy Puppy went careening down the hall toward the kitchen. Michelle zipped it shut and slung the bag over her shoulder. It has better not be Rob whose boots were making the old floor creak, she thought grimly. Shoving the adjoining door open she followed the dogs into the room.

"What are you doing, Michelle?" Cale's gaze raked over the bag on her shoulder.

"Leaving, like I told you," she said stubbornly and made to go around him. "I don't want to crowd you and Stacey." She flung the words at him.

Anger darkened his face. "It wasn't me rolling around on the floor half dressed with my ex," he countered. "And I've told you a hun—"

"Ha! So you finally admit that the blonde bimbo is your ex." Anger and something she couldn't name built in her gut making it hard to breathe.

"That's not what I said, for God's sake." He paused and took a deep breath. "Can we just sit down and talk about this like two adults instead of trading insults?" Cale ran a hand through his hair.

"What's there to talk about? You don't trust me. C'mon, dogs." She stepped by him.

He caught her arm to stop her. "You're not seriously considering taking the dogs with you, are you?"

"They're mine, of course I'm taking them."

"Michelle, don't be stupid. Shut up in that little trailer is no place for those two. You know that. Leave them here."

"They're mine," she repeated.

"I'm not saying they're not. I'm just asking you to be sensible and think of them for a minute."

"I have to take them with me. I'll miss them if I don't…they'll miss me."

"You know where they are and it's not like I'm gonna change the locks on you," he countered. "They're happy here, this is where they think home is."

Storm sat down with a thump and leaned against Cale's leg, her eyes fixed on Michelle's.

Even Crazy Puppy sat still and gazed up at the man with adoring eyes. The dog's outline blurred through the moisture gathering in her eyes. "I suppose you're right," she admitted. "I just feel like I'm abandoning them somehow."

"You could just stay." Cale dipped his head and didn't look at her.

"I don't know, Cale. Maybe we need to spend some time apart. We kinda jumped into this relationship pretty quick and if you actually think I'd go running back to Rob…"

He scrubbed a hand across the stubble on his chin. "What am I supposed to think when he keeps showing up wherever you are all the time? You don't seem to be able to say no to the guy."

"You're supposed to trust me. I can't control what the jackass does or says. You're right on one count. I'm through rescuing him when he gets himself in trouble. That's Kayla's job now."

"I'm glad to hear you say that, Michelle. It's a start." He raised his head and met her gaze. "We can't work this out if we aren't talking to each other. I have no problem with you stayin here."

"In the spare room?" She bit her lip.

"That might be better. We need to fix the trust issue without muddling it up. Just because we're physically attracted to each other, making love won't make the underlying problems go away."

Disappointment seared through her. Being careful to keep her expression neutral Michelle considered his words. Unable to come up with a satisfactory decision she slid the bag off her shoulder and set it on a chair. "I'll have to think on it, Cale. Rob was trying to rape me for God's sake and all you did was tell me to get inside and cover up. Don't you think I was upset and could have used a bit of comfort?"

"I'm sorry, Michelle. I…"

"Look, I'll call you later. I'm late. I told Pat I'd be there by ten. I've got the arena to myself until noon if I want it." She picked up the bag and started for the door.

"At least leave the dogs here for the time being," Cale suggested.

"I guess that is the best thing for them," she conceded. "I will call you later, once I'm finished at Prairie Winds."

Cale didn't let go of her arm but pulled her toward him and planted a kiss on her lips. "I do love you, Michelle." He released her.

Somewhat bemused, she regained her composure enough to answer. "I love you too, but love isn't what's in question here. Trust is. I'll call you later," she promised again.

Cale stepped aside and Michelle moved toward the door. She pushed it open and glanced behind her. Cale was just disappearing through the opposite door with the dogs close on his heels. She shifted the heavy carry all; maybe she should just leave it here? But then again, maybe not. The stubborn streak was strong in her and it wouldn't let her give in to her longing to accept Cale's overture.

She closed the door behind her and strode across the yard. After throwing the carryall into the back seat she stepped up into the cab and started the engine. Leaving it running she went into the barn to get Spud and Rain. Haltering both horses, she led them down the aisle and into the yard. She stopped to close and latch the barn door and then continued to the back of the rig. The horses waited patiently for her to open the trailer door. Michelle threw the shank over Spud's withers and clicked for him to go ahead and load. The gelding pushed his nose against her in search of a treat, when none was forthcoming he sighed and stepped up into the trailer. Rain stood quietly while Michelle hopped up and closed the stall divider while still holding the lead shank. She got back down and looped the shank over the mare's withers and gave her a bit of tug before letting go. The mare obediently got in and Michelle secured the door. She went around the side and opened the hatch in front of both horses. She clipped both halters to their respective ties with a panic snap and closed the hatch again.

In short order she was rolling out the lane and past the coulee. She spared a thought for how Stacey was managing with the chores and helping out at the clinic as well. George should be home middle of next week, that should take some of the burden off. Maybe then the woman would stop hanging around Cale at the clinic.

Although, the help was a God send. Poor Harvey couldn't fill in on a regular basis and Michelle would have to miss a few rodeos until Doc was feeling better unless she could arrange coverage.

The traffic was light on the highway when she turned onto the hardtop. She headed south and cranked the country station on the radio. The turnoff to Pat's was just up ahead. Michelle signaled and slowed for the turn, being careful not to put the horses off balance. Gravel growled beneath the tires and even though it was April dust swirled in the wake of her passing. *We better get some moisture soon or hay is gonna be through the roof this year.* There was still a chance of a good yield if the rain came at the right time. No sense worrying about something that hadn't happened yet, as Grampa always said. There was enough to worry over already.

Prairie Winds arena lay nestled in a small valley, the sun glinting off the metal roof when she crested the next hill.

Michelle loved the spring time. Time to start gearing up for the season. She'd missed the indoor show at Medicine Hat, it was the coming weekend and Spud wasn't quite up to speed yet. She could have taken Rain just for the experience, but it really wasn't worth the gas and other fees to go with just one horse. Besides there was the High River Winter Series sanctioned by the Alberta Barrel Racing Association. She planned to run Rain in the time only section and then enter Spud in the Jackpot. He'd done well at the last one in March and she had high hopes for a top three finish next weekend.

Pat came out of the barn at the sound of the truck tires on the gravel. She waved and waited for Michelle to pull up into the area to the side to unload. She turned off the truck and opened the door. "Hey Pat, how's it going?"

"Good. What's with the text about needing a hook up for the trailer? Things not so rosy with the hunky vet?" Pat grinned at her while helping unlatch the end gate of the trailer.

"Yeah, we had a bit of a misunderstanding," Michelle prevaricated. "It'll blow over. I was just pissed when I texted you and wanted to be sure I had a place to crash if I needed it."

"Misunderstanding? Sounded more like you and Rob were having a flashback. Can't blame Cale for not appreciating finding you two rolling around on the floor of his kitchen."

"Seriously? I see the gossip grapevine is working well. Where'd you hear it from?"

"Your ex was belly aching about it at the hotel while trying to drown his sorrows. At the top of his lungs. He shut up pretty quick when that little wife of his showed up and dragged him out by the ear. You ready to unload these guys?" Pat waited to open the gate until Michelle nodded.

"So everybody knows. Damn Rob and his big mouth. Huh, I've got better things to do than worry about that right now. Let's get these guys off and run some barrels." She went around to the side and unhooked the trailer tie through the side hatch. Coming back around to the end gate she unlatched the divider and let Rain come off, grabbing the lead shank from her withers as the horse went past. Pat took the mare and tied her to the side of the trailer while Michelle opened the divider and unhook Spud's tie. With her hand on his shoulder she guided him off the trailer and tied him alongside Rain.

"I'm gonna tack up here, save dragging everything into the barn." She busied herself with brushes and hoof pick. "I'll meet you in the arena in fifteen minutes or so."

"Sounds good. I'll go get Caramel tacked up. She's full of beans this morning." Pat grinned and headed to the barn.

Michelle groomed and tacked the horses in short order and stowed the equipment in the trailer. Leaving Spud tied to the trailer with a blanket over him, she brought Rain to the arena.

"Door!" She waited a moment. There was nothing more annoying or dangerous than having someone open a door when a horse was going by it.

"Clear!" Pat's voice was muffled by the door.

Michelle opened the man door which was wide enough for a horse with tack on to come through safely. It saved cranking open the large main door. She led Rain through and turned to close the door behind her. Pausing for a minute to allow her eyes to adjust to the dimmer lighting in the arena, her hands automatically checked the tightness of the horse's girth and fit of the bridle. There was no reason to expect the bridle needed adjusting, but it was just habit, something ingrained in her by Grampa. Something along the lines of the parachuting maxim of always packing your own chute. Blinking a little Michelle brought the horse off the track into the centre of the building. Pat was working Caramel at a lope on the rail. The horse went along at a relaxed pace, head low and stretching out her frame. Michelle grinned, once that mare knew it was time to turn some barrels she was a firecracker and all business. She tightened her girth a notch, slipped the reins over Rain's head and stepped up into the saddle. The quarter horse danced sideways and snorted. She slid a hand down the sleek hide of the neck and nudged the mare into a walk. After a few circuits of the arena in both directions she picked up a trot, allowing the horse to move out and not confining her to a jog. By the time Michelle had warmed up to a lope, Pat had pulled into the centre of the arena and dismounted to check her girth before moving on to the fast work of running the cloverleaf barrel pattern. She waited until Michelle turned in and halted beside her.

"You want to run first?" Michelle swung down from Rain and patted the mare's neck. "I'm just gonna take is slow with this one."

"Sure, time me, will you?" Pat tossed her a stop watch.

"You're on." Michelle led Rain to the side of the arena opposite the start line for the pattern. Pat already had the barrels set up at the regulation measurements. She envied her friend the large building and wished she had the money to build one out at the ranch.

"Ready?" Pat turned her horse's back to the start line and the little horse pranced and half-reared in her eagerness to run.

"When you are." Michelle held her finger over the start button on the stop watch and aligned herself with the white limed start line. The time probable wouldn't be as accurate as using the automatic timers they employed at events but it would certainly give both women a ball park time.

Pat whirled around and Caramel leaped forward. Michelle pressed the button as they flashed by the start. Pat ran the pattern taking the right hand barrel first which gave her two left turns on the last two barrels. The rules stated a rider could take either of the top two barrels first. Michelle preferred the left barrel first, especially with Spud. Horses tend to turn in one direction easier than the other, much like some people were right handed and some left. Caramel's breathing echoed in the enclosed space as she ran for home. Michelle stopped the clock when the horse's nose broke the finish/start line.

The mare danced and snorted as Pat pulled her up. "How'd we do?"

"Nineteen-one-four."

"Not as fast as I'd like." Pat grimaced. "I missed my mark going into the first barrel and missed it again on the way to the second." She swung down from the saddle, unclipped the rein and handed the end to Michelle. "Here, can you hold her while I put more flour on my marks?"

"Sure." She took the short rein and stroked Caramel's nose. The little mare was hardly blowing at all. "She sure in great shape for this time of year," she remarked.

Pat came back dusting her hands free of excess flour. "Yeah, we've been doing a lot of hills and outside work when the footing has been good. Not a lot of moisture this spring so the trails are all clear." She took Caramel's rein back and the stop watch as well. "Your turn."

Michelle slid the rein over her horse's neck and mounted. "I'm just gonna trot the pattern a few times and then lope it if she stays on track at the trot." She grinned. "No need to time me." She touched the mare with her heel and took her to the centre line of the arena, turning her back to the pattern. Once they could practice outside, she'd introduce her to coming into the outdoor arena through a wide chute at a full gallop. She'd need to be comfortable with that before Michelle took her to the outdoor events where the infield was set up for barrel racing and the horses could enter at the run through a chute.

She rode the clover leaf pattern five or six times at the trot and then picked up an easy lope. She halted after circling the outside of the arena once and turned the mare's nose to the overhead door again. This time when they came around and headed for the first barrel Michelle let the mare lope. She was careful to keep the same distance from the barrel as they had at the trot. It was so important the horse learn where her feet should fall and be consistent no matter what speed. She repeated the exercise four times and then pulled up by Pat.

"I think that's enough for Rain. I'll walk her out a bit while you warm up again." She reached down and took the stop watch.

"Thanks. She looks good. You might have another winner on your hands if she keeps going the way she is." Pat swung up into the saddle.

"It'd be nice. Even if we only win day money and not the aggregate it sure helps going down the road."

"You got that right," her friend called over her shoulder as she trotted away.

Pat ran the pattern a few more times. Michelle took Rain out to the trailer while Pat put her horse away. Michelle untacked the mare, brushed the sweat marks away and checked her hooves before blanketing her and loading her on the trailer. She returned to the arena with Spud. Pat met her inside the door to act as timer.

Spud was an old hand and knew the pattern as well or better than his rider. After a brief warmup to loosen and stretch his muscles, they ran the pattern a few times. Michelle pulled up after the last run and slapped his neck in appreciation. "Good man!"

"Eighteen-nine-three. Not bad." Pat reported.

"We'll have to pick it up a bit. Lisa won Calgary last year with a seventeen-nine-o-seven."

"Can't worry about that. Just run to beat your own best time," Pat advised.

"I guess." Michelle stepped down off Spud. She threw the left stirrup over the saddle and loosened his girth. The gelding was hardly blowing at all, a sure sign that he was in good shape. "I'll take him out and untack at the trailer."

"Why don't you just put them in a couple of stalls here? It'll save you trailering them over every day. You were gonna do that anyway before hunky Doctor Cale managed to change your mind this morning," Pat said.

Michelle wheeled around. "How did you know I changed my mind?"

"Friends know things." She smirked. "And you didn't pull the trailer up by the electrical hookup."

"Yeah, well." Michelle had the grace to blush.

"Nothin' wrong with a change of heart, girl. You'd be a fool to let that man get away. Here, let me take Spud and you go get Rain off the trailer. There's room in the tack room for your gear. I'll untack him for you, just bring his blanket in."

"Thanks, Pat. That will make things less complicated for sure." She slipped out the man door and crossed the graveled lot to the trailer. Rain was waiting patiently munching on her hay. Michelle unhooked her tie, opened the divider and led her back off the trailer. This time she used the sliding barn door rather than entering the arena. Spud was already in a stall with his blanket on and a pile of hay in front of him. She put Rain in the stall beside him and slid the door shut.

"Thanks for taking care of Spud."

"Anytime. Just write what you want them to get fed on the board in the feed room. I left you two saddle racks in the tack room and there's plenty of space to store your other gear. I gotta run, but I'll see you tomorrow, right?" Pat stopped with her hand on the door.

"You bet, same time as today unless you text me with something different. I'll be out of your hair as soon as I drag the rest of my stuff in."

"I'd help you but I've got an appointment in town." Pat waved and left.

It only took Michelle a few minutes to transfer her things into the barn. After checking to be sure the two horses were settled and comfortable, she jotted down the feed instructions on the board in the feed room and went to unhook the trailer. First, she pulled it up close to the hook up and plugged the electricity in. Unhooking took a few minutes more and then she was pulling out of the yard and pointing the nose of the truck for home.

Home. Yes, home was no longer her childhood home. Home was wherever Cale was, no matter where that took her.

Chapter Seven

The drive home took less time without the trailer. She stopped at the clinic and forced a smile on her face before she went in. No doubt Stacey would be ensconced behind the reception desk. Michelle checked her phone but there was no message from Mary. *Might be good, might be bad.* Maybe Cale would have heard something. She pushed the door open and let herself in. The bell over the door jangled, and sure enough, Stacey poked her head out of the back.

"Michelle, am I ever glad to see you," the blonde greeted her.

"Why?" Michelle blinked in surprise. It certainly wasn't the reception she was expecting.

"There's this dog with porcupine quills…Cale got called out on an emergency…" Tears shone in the woman's china blue eyes.

"Why are you dealing with it? Where's the vet tech?"

"Caleb quit this morning."

"What? He just quit with no notice?" Michelle shook her head.

"He got a call to go work on the rigs and well, you know, the money's a lot better than working here."

"I guess, but talk about burning your bridges. Where's the dog's owner?" Michelle glanced around the waiting room.

"Don't know. Some guy came in and said he found the dog by the side of the road. Dumped him and left in big hurry."

"Figures." She added a few curse words. "So you're trying to pull the quills by yourself?"

"I just feel so bad for him. I just couldn't leave him in a kennel crying like that and pawing at his face. But I can't get a grip on the damn things and he keeps wriggling around."

"Did you call Cale and let him know?"

Stacey nodded. "I did, but he's way down by Stavely. He said to leave it til he got back, but the poor dog keeps crying and…"

"Yeah, I know. I can't stand to hear them cry either. Okay, let's go see what we can do for him."

A short time and a few tubes of teething gel later the quills that weren't broken off were removed and the dog was resting quietly. Michelle poured two mugs of coffee and handed one to Stacey. The two women sat in companionable silence.

"I was never so glad to see anybody come through the door," Stacey broke the silence.

"Huh, really?" Michelle snorted.

"Really. I knew you'd know what to do. George is always on about Michelle would have done this or Michelle would have done that. Nothing I do seems to be right." The blonde bit her bottom lip.

"That's a switch." She laughed. "My brother is never happy with the way I do things. At least that's what he says every time he comes home."

Stacey giggled. "Maybe it's just a guy thing?"

"Or an idiot thing." Michelle joined in the laughter. She got up and set the empty mug on the corner of the reception desk. "You want some help cleaning up here? I've got to get home, but I can spare some time to clear up this mess."

"You go on. There's not much here and I've got to stay until five anyway. Have you heard from Mary today?"

Michelle shook her head. "No, but if she's up at the hospital with Doc she won't be looking at her phone. I'm gonna try her though." She dug in her pocket for the phone. Pushing the speed dial she waited while it connected. "Damn, it went right to voice mail. I'll try her again when I get home and let you know if I hear anything."

"I'd appreciate it, Michelle. I still feel like an outsider here and I don't want to bother Mary too much. I'm not sure how much she likes me." Colour rose in the woman's cheeks staining her fair skin red.

"Don't worry about Mary. She loves everyone, especially if there's a chance she might get to play matchmaker. The woman has been trying to get that brother of mine settled down for years. She probably thinks you're a God send."

"Really?"

"For sure. He has never, and I mean never, let one of his conquests move into the ranch. He even surprised me when he asked you to stay."

"I thought he did that just to piss you off."

"It did piss me off, but he wouldn't risk his freedom just to aggravate me. Seems the lunkhead must really care for you." Michelle shook her head. "Who knew?"

"Does this mean you don't hate me anymore?" Stacey cocked her head to one side and met Michelle's gaze.

"I don't hate you." She had the grace to blush and feel ashamed. "It's just, well you know about Rob and how he…"

"I've heard the gossip, for sure. But from what I've seen recently, you're better off without him."

"You got that right. But it doesn't make me the most trusting soul on the planet. He really blindsided me when he disappeared and came back married. I mean, crap, I couldn't drag him to the altar even though we'd been engaged forever. And then…Wham. Back he comes with a pretty little dressage queen wife in tow."

"Honest, Michelle. Cale and I are just friends. I've known him for a really long time. And, yeah, maybe I used to think about what it would be like to be more than friends." She paused and held up a hand at the change in Michelle's expression. "Hear me out. He just

93

doesn't think of me in that way. Cale sees me like a little sister, and after meeting your brother I have to say Cale was smarter than I am. He was right all along when he told me he wasn't the one for me."

"You think George is? He's like your knight in shining armour?" Michelle was hard put not to burst out laughing.

"He is, Michelle. You might find it funny, but when Peggy introduced me to him last Christmas…I don't know how to explain it…it felt like I'd known him all my life. He's a hard man to get to know. Like he has all these walls I have to get around…"

'In his defense, my brother has had to be the man of the house since Dad died and I haven't always made it easy for him. He's had to live up to Dad's expectations for years and he worshiped Grampa. Dad was kind of tough on him 'cause he was the oldest and his only son."

Stacey nodded. "He said something like that when we were talking one time. He felt he could never be as good as your dad and he was jealous of you because your father thought you walked on water and couldn't do anything wrong in his eyes."

"He told you that?" Michelle's eyebrows rose incredulously. "How drunk was he?"

"Stone cold sober."

"Wow. You must have really got to him. Well, good luck to you, I say." Michelle shook her head. "You sure I can't help you clean up here?"

"Nope, I'm good. You go on."

"Don't you have chores to do at home? It'll be dark before you get there."

"George is home today. He should be there before me and he said he take care of them."

"Oh, I didn't realize he was coming home today. I haven't heard from him lately."

"We talk every day. I don't think he's sure of his reception if he called you. He asks about you all the time."

"I guess I can't blame him. Maybe I'll try and come over while he's home this time. No guarantees we won't try to kill each other though."

Stacey's laughter followed Michelle out the door. She turned and stuck her head back in. "Tell Cale I'll see him at home."

"Will do." Stacey waved and disappeared into the back of the clinic.

Michelle closed the door and strode to her truck. Once in the cab she started the engine and paused to redial Mary. She almost hung up on the fourth ring when Mary answered.

"Chelly?"

"Hey, Mary. You still in Calgary?"

"I just left Luke. He's doing good. Being his cantankerous old self, giving those poor nurses grief."

"I can only imagine." Michelle laughed. "Any idea when he can come home?"

"That nice young doctor said maybe day after tomorrow, as long as he behaves himself."

"That's a relief. It'll be nice to have him back where he belongs. Are you still staying at Emma's?"

"I am. She's been a dear, driving me back and forth and making sure I eat. I don't know what I'd do without her."

"Good friends are hard to come by. When you get the go ahead to spring Doc give me a call and I'll come pick you up and bring you home."

"Thanks, Chelly. Luke and I really appreciate it. I hear Stacey's been filling in at the clinic." There was a question behind Mary's words.

Michelle grinned. "Don't worry, Mary. I haven't scalped her or anything...yet."

"Michelle!"

"Just kidding, woman. Honestly, we actually had a civilized conversation this afternoon. She really seems to be hooked on my idiot brother. Go figure."

"I'm glad you're finally being reasonable about her. From what I've seen she's not a bad person at all. Things okay between you and Cale? Luke talked to him earlier today and said the boy sounded upset about something."

"We had a bit of a set to earlier, but things will be okay. I'm headed home now. We'll work it out, Mary. Tell Doc not to worry about anything but getting better. The clinic is doing fine and so are the rest of us. Stacey says George is home today, by the way."

"You need to mend fences with him too, Chelly."

"We'll see. No promises. Look, I gotta go. Give Doc my love and call me the minute you know anything."

"Be nice to poor Cale, Chelly. The boy does love you. Don't blow it, he's the best thing that ever happened to you. Talk to you later."

"You make me sound like the wicked witch of the west, Mary. I love him too, you know…" She broke off when the connection was lost. "Dammit!"

Tossing the phone on the passenger seat she slid the truck into gear and pulled onto the hardtop. She was still mulling over what to say to Cale when she passed the Wilson ranch lane. The lights were on in the barn and the house so George must have made it home already. She resisted the urge to turn down the familiar drive. Let Stacey and George have tonight for themselves. She wasn't sure what she would say to him anyway, or if he even wanted to speak to her. Minutes later she parked in the yard at Cale's. The sound of Storm and Crazy Puppy barking carried through the walls. She grinned at the sight of Crazy Puppy with his face smushed against the kitchen window, huge paws gripping the narrow sill.

"Coming, mutts. Pipe down!"

Wasting no time, she crossed the yard and let the dogs out. The puppy bounced everywhere, his tail waving over his back while Storm much more sedately went about doing her business. The wind had picked up when the sun went down, Michelle shivered as it howled in the overhead wires. She whistled for the dogs and let them in before following them, shutting the door firmly on the cold dark.

Flicking on the lights Michelle started a pot of coffee and then filled the dog bowls with food and water, setting them back on the floor. While the coffee brewed she contemplated what to make for dinner. A glance at the clock said it was almost six. *Should I call him and see if he's left Stavely yet?* She was suddenly shy about contacting him. *Maybe I'll just make a casserole, it'll keep in the oven until Cale comes home.* Ignoring the nagging little voice at the back of her mind that whispered she was taking the coward's way out, she pulled ground beef out of the freezer and popped it into the microwave to thaw.

Still no sign of Cale by seven o'clock. The casserole was in the oven keeping warm, she'd done what washing up there was and swept the floor clear of dog hair. Michelle cradled the hot coffee mug between her hands and rested her elbows on the table. Across the coulee the lights were out in the big barn so George must have finished chores. *I wonder if Stacey is home yet? She should be by now, the roads are clear.* Again, she resisted the urge to dial the familiar number.

Unable to sit still a minute longer, she pushed back the chair and took her coffee into the office. Might as well do some invoicing and paper work while she waited. Storm and Crazy Puppy followed her and settled down by her feet. She stroked the puppy's head while she waited for the program to boot up.

"Michelle! Are you here?" Cale's voice broke her concentration while she was struggling to make hide nor hair of the scribbled notes.

"In the office." The dogs scrambled to their feet and charged into the kitchen to greet him. Michelle stood and stretched to ease the kink in her back and followed more slowly. She paused in the doorway to the kitchen. "Long day?"

"It was that," he agreed.

"Did you stop by the clinic before you came home?"

Cale dropped into a chair by the table and shook his head. "Nope, I'm beat. Just wanted to get home, eat, and crash."

"Stacey called you about that dog didn't she?"

"The reception sucked. All I could decipher was that someone dropped off a stray dog?"

"A stray dog with a face full of quills."

"Shit! I really don't want to go back to the clinic, but I can't leave the poor thing with a face full of quills. Any in the eyes?" Cale pushed himself upright and crossed the room to pour coffee into a travel mug.

"He's probably okay until morning. Stacey and I managed to remove the obvious ones. There are some that are broken off, but none in the eyes."

"Cale leaned a hip on the counter and regarded her over the rim of the mug as he took a huge swig. "Let me get this straight. You and Stacey actually worked together? She isn't stuffed in the freezer at the clinic or something?"

Heat suffused Michelle's face. "I guess I deserve that. We were both so worried about the poor dog we just did what needed to be done."

Cale crossed back to the table and sat down, leaning his head on one hand. "God, I'm tired. Have you heard from Mary? How's Doc?"

Michelle busied herself pulling the casserole out of the oven and piling a heaping serving on a plate. She put it in front of Cale, added bread, butter and ketchup to the table along with a knife and fork. She took the chair opposite him. "Doc is doing good. Mary says he might be able to come home in the next day or two if he behaves himself."

"Now that is good news." Cale lifted his head and grinned at her. Silence filled the kitchen while he applied himself to clearing his plate. Pushing the dish aside he leaned back and rubbed his eyes. "I wasn't sure you'd be here when I got home. Where's the trailer?"

"I left the horses and the trailer at Pat's. I'm still not thrilled that you could think I was encouraging Rob, but if we're gonna make this thing work, we need to talk it out."

"I agree. Do you want to start, or should I?" Cale got up and poured fresh coffee for both of them and returned to the table.

"I don't understand why you think I'm still interested in Rob. I'm here with you and I keep telling you I love you." Michelle swirled the coffee in her cup and ignored the tears prickling the backs of her eyes.

"Look at it from my point of view. Every time the guy gets in a jam he calls you to bail him out. Instead of saying no and letting his wife handle it, you go running to his rescue. This latest episode is just the last in a long line. It's like he's a habit you can't break. The whole town is just sitting back and waiting to see how long it will take before he dumps Kayla and you dump me and go running back to him."

Michelle raised her head and met his gaze. "Okay, you're right. I should never have gone to Okotoks and saved his ass. I should have called Kayla and let her deal with it. I won't make that mistake again. As for what the gossips are saying...I can't control what they say or think. Those old boys at the hotel will bet on anything. I can only assure you that I have no intention of dumping you. Even if we can't make this work between us, there is no way in hell I will ever go back to Rob Chetwynd. And while we're on that subject, when are you going to change the name on the ranch gate?"

"The new sign is on order. Should be here be the end of May at the latest. Okay, my turn. You've got this ridiculous notion in your head that I'm attracted to Stacey. I have no idea where that came from. We went out a couple of

101

times in high school. That was it, nothing ever came of it."

"Have you seen the way she looks at you?" Michelle's voice rose incredulously.

Cale heaved a sigh and lifted one shoulder in a half shrug. "She may have been harbouring some hope of trying to re-ignite an old flame when she showed up here, I give you that. But it was all purely on her side and after she met your brother...well, as far as being her love interest I've just faded into the background."

"So you don't have any regrets about what might have been. No lingering feelings?" Michelle cocked her head to one side and worried her bottom lip.

"No regrets as far as Stacey is concerned. She's my friend and so of course I have feelings for her. But not the kind you mean. Let me ask you, do you still have feelings for Rob? Still love him?"

She frowned and opened her mouth to protest.

"Think about it before you go off half-cocked," Cale cautioned.

Michelle snapped her mouth shut and wrestled with her indignation. "Okay, I get your point. Of course I still have feelings for Rob. On some level I will always love him, but not the way I love you. And I promise I will try very hard to be nicer to Stacey in the future and not to let my imagination run away with me." She paused. "She's just so damned pretty and I'm, well, I'm just me." She flapped a hand at herself indicating the worn jeans, flannel shirt and hair every which way.

Cale got up, catching her hand and pulling her upright with him. "I think you're the most beautiful woman I've ever seen." He wrapped his arms around her and kissed her. "Is this stupid fight over? Can we get back to being as normal as we ever are?" He grinned.

Michelle savoured the strength of his arms around her and buried her face in his neck. "Let's never fight again, okay?" Cale's laughter rumbled in her ear and he kissed the top of her head.

"You're you and I'm me, I don't think I can promise we'll never have another argument. Just promise to never run away from me again. There's nothing we can't work out if we just stick together."

"Promise." Michelle kissed the side of his neck and trailed her lips up to his ear.

"Wench," He chuckled and swung her up into his arms.

She giggled and hung on tight as he crossed the room and shouldered the door open. They made it to the bedroom only bouncing off the walls of the narrow hall twice. Cale lowered her to the bed and stretched out beside her not bothering to turn on the light.

"The dogs need to go out…"

Cale silenced her with his lips and then lifted his head, eyes gleaming in the dim light from the window. "The dogs can wait until morning. With any luck the damn phone won't ring with an emergency."

"Did you hear from Carrie?" Michelle tried to raise herself on one elbow.

"Forget the clinic, and the dogs. Concentrate on this." Cale proceeded to kiss her thoroughly, his hands roaming over her body as he removed her shirt and jeans.

Crazy Puppy uttered a yelp of protest when the clothing fell off the bed. Michelle giggled and gave herself up to Cale's love making.

Chapter Eight

The truck tires hummed on the pavement and Michelle sang along with the radio. The bright sunlight picking out the jewel green of spring grass exactly matched her mood. Doc was ready to come home and she was only too happy to make the drive to Calgary to collect him and Mary. Harvey was back at the house giving it a good cleaning and replenishing the contents of the fridge and pantry. Stacey was helping when the clinic wasn't busy. Michelle grinned. She had to give the devil her due, the woman was more than helpful. Maybe it was time to bury the hatchet, and not between the woman's pretty little ears. It would certainly make Cale happy.

A frown creased her forehead. Although, there was still George to consider. She hadn't had a chance to talk to him since he'd been home. Frankly, she'd avoided it like the plague. It was obvious he wasn't going to make the first move and her pride insisted she shouldn't either. *Damn Wilson stubbornness.* That's what Doc would say, all right. Maybe she'd call her brother once she got Doc and Mary home and settled. Maybe.

Pushing the problem to the back of her mind, Michelle concentrated on the busy Calgary traffic. She hated Sixteenth Avenue, too many stop lights and way too many cars. Damned cyclists, too. The lanes were not made to accommodate a big pickup and a bike lane too. She gritted her teeth when a cyclist zipped through a cross walk still mounted, while she idled at a red light. Cyclists seemed to think they were exempt from the rules of the road. *Shouldn't tar them all with the same brush, I suppose.* There were some responsible ones, it was just the idiots who stuck in her mind.

Shaking her head, she turned left at Twenty-ninth Street and then into Foothills Medical Centre. She intended to go past the main entrance and find a parking spot in the upper lot. As she passed the main entrance Mary waved her down. Michelle stomped on the brake and wedged the truck into the little layby just past the busy sliding doors. Leaving the vehicle running she jumped out and came around the front of the truck.

"For the love of God, woman, let me out of this damned chair," Doc bellowed.

Mary disregarded him and continued pushing the wheelchair along the sidewalk. She had to skirt the ambulatory patients who crowded the benches along the walkway. Some sneaking a smoke and some just enjoying the spring sunshine.

"Shut up, old man," Mary chided her husband and ignored his attempts to get his feet on the ground and stand up. "Hello, Chelly. As you can see, the old goat is feeling more like his old self." Mary came to a halt by the passenger side of the truck.

"I can see that." It was all she could do to keep from laughing out loud. "Let's get you in the back then." She opened the rear door of the club cab.

"I ain't ridin' in the back like an invalid," Doc grumbled and crossed his arms over his chest.

"You ride where we say, or so help me I'll leave you right here," Mary warned her husband.

"C'mon, Doc. How can Mary and I gossip if she's not in the front? You know you hate listening to us natter."

"Luke," Mary's tone brooked no argument.

"Fine!" He heaved a huge sigh. "Women. I can't win against the both of you."

Doc struggled without success to rise out of the chair. Mary engaged the brake and slipped her hand under his elbow. Michelle did the same on the opposite side. He got upright on unsteady feet.

"Damned embarrassing when a man can't even stand up on his own," he complained.

"Now, Luke, there's nobody here to see you. Let's get you into the truck, shall we? You'll feel better once you get home," Mary attempted to sooth her husband.

Between the two women they got him settled in the truck and Mary tucked a blanket around his legs. "Quit coddling me, for God's sake."

"Humour me, old man." Mary patted his knee and closed the door.

Michelle grinned and went around to the driver's side. She had to wait for a break in the flow of traffic before she could pull out. "Damn, this place is busy. Does it ever slow down?"

"Not that I've seen," Mary said.

"Do we need to stop at Emma's and pick up anything?" Michelle deftly took advantage of a taxi stopping in the lane by the main doors to discharge a passenger, effectively stopping traffic.

"No, I have it all here." Mary patted the large bag she had unlooped from the back of the wheelchair and thrown in the truck earlier.

"Home we go then." Michelle turned east on Sixteenth Avenue and headed toward the Deerfoot. "Shit, I hate this traffic. I don't know how people stand this every day."

"I guess they just get used to it," Mary replied. She nodded toward the back seat.

Michelle took a quick look in the rearview mirror. Doc's head rested on the side of the door, eyes closed and tiny snores emanating from his slack mouth. "Wish I had time to take a picture of that." She giggled.

"Tempting as that is, he'd never forgive us." Mary grinned.

Once they were clear of the south end of Calgary, Michelle picked up speed. The two women spent the rest of the drive talking of inconsequential things. As they left the number Two Highway near Aldersyde and took

Highway 7 west toward Black Diamond, Michelle caught Mary looking at her with a calculating expression on her face.

"What's that look for?"

"I want to ask you something, but it's really none of my business."

Michelle snorted. "When did that ever stop you before? Ask away. Can't promise I'll answer though."

"How are things with you and Cale? Did you work out whatever was going on?"

"I might have known that matchmaking would be the first thing on your mind." Michelle laughed. "Yes, we talked it out and everything's fine."

"So what happens if Rob sends out an SOS again?" Mary narrowed her eyes.

"He's SOL. Kayla can take care of him. I'm done." She glanced over at her friend. "I mean it, don't give me that look."

"I'm glad to hear it. Just stick to your guns." Mary settled back in her seat and nodded.

Michelle slowed at the outskirts of the little town of Black Diamond. "Do you want a coffee or anything?"

Mary glanced toward the back seat where Doc was still sleeping. "No, let's just keep going and get him home where he belongs."

"Works for me." She turned south on Highway Twenty-two at the centre of town. Once she was clear of the town limits she accelerated. The rolling prairie on either side of the road stretched away to the west where the mountains reared their snowy heads against the bright blue sky. The sight made her heart sing. There was nothing like springtime in Alberta after a long cold winter.

"Does a body good, doesn't it?" Mary nodded out her window at the passing vista.

"I wouldn't want to live anywhere else in the world," Michelle agreed. The truck rolled down the sloping hill at the north end of Longview. "Home sweet home, here we are." In minutes she pulled into the lane at the back of the house.

"Wake up, Luke, we're home." Mary turned and laid her hand on her husband's knee.

"Whaa…?" Doc's eyelids fluttered and he wiped a shaky hand across his mouth. "What? Where are we?" He struggled into a more upright position.

"We're home, Luke. Just take your time to wake up." His wife got out of the truck and opened the rear door. "Here, let me move this blanket. Just wait til you're awake, no sense falling and ending up back at the hospital."

Michelle came around the rear of the truck and stopped beside Mary. "What can I do to help?"

"I heard you were coming. Glad to see you home, you old coot." Harvey almost ran down the walk from the back door of the clinic. "I thought I saw you go by the clinic a minute a go."

"Who you callin' an old coot, you reprobate?" Doc brightened up at the sight of his old friend and neighbor. "Get out of the way, woman. Let a man have a little room. I can get out of a truck on my own steam, for heaven's sake."

Harvey winked at Michelle and moved to help Doc out of the truck. "C'mon, I've got the coffee on and some sandwiches on the table." He supported Doc under the pretense of putting a neighborly arm around the other man's shoulders. "It's decaf," he mouthed the words to Mary as he passed her.

"I'm just gonna duck into the clinic and see if Cale is there before I come in." Michelle squeezed her friend's arm and headed for the rear door of the clinic. She hesitated before she went it and glanced toward the house. Mary followed Doc and Harvey inside and closed the door. Michelle pushed open the clinic door and entered the meds room.

"Cale? You here?"

"I thought I heard the door." Stacey stuck her head in from the reception area. "Cale's in surgery."

"I just wanted to let him know Doc is home. Will you let him know when he's done?"

"Sure. How is Doctor Cassidy?"

"He's fine. Or as fine as can be expected, I guess. Do you really call him Doctor Cassidy to his face?" She smothered a giggle.

Stacey nodded. "I don't know what else I should call him. I don't know him well enough to call him Luke or Doc."

"Everyone calls him Doc. You'll give him a big head if you keep calling him Doctor Cassidy." Michelle grinned.

"As long as you're sure he won't mind." Stacey tipped her head to one side.

"Just call him Doc, please. I'm gonna go make sure Mary doesn't need anything, then I'm headed home."

"I think Harvey has everything under control. He's been like a mouse on a hot brick all day, just waiting for you guys to get back. What a dear man he is."

"Yeah, he is a sweetie," Michelle agreed. "How are you and George making out?"

A pretty flush spread over the blonde's face. "It's good. Everything's good," she stammered.

"Like that, is it?" Michelle grinned.

"It's just weird talking about it with his sister."

"I could tell you a few stories, but I'll spare you the gory details for now. See you later." She left the clinic and cut across the bit of lawn to the back door of the house. She peeked in the window before going in. Harvey and Doc were at the table and Mary was bustling around her kitchen. *Everything back to normal.* A weight Michelle hadn't actively been aware of lifted from her shoulders. *Thank you, God for not taking him away from me.* "Hey, it's so good to see you home, Doc." She came into the kitchen.

"Chelly, come sit down." Doc waved a hand at an empty chair. "It's good to be home.

Stupid hospitals, a man can't get a decent night's sleep what with them rattling and clattering around. I mean, who in their right mind comes into a man's room at midnight, wakes him up and proceeds to take his vitals?"

"You're home now, Luke. Don't get yourself all upset." Mary laid a hand on his arm.

"Hospital ain't a good place for a sick man. All that pokin' and proddin' and them flappin' night shirts." Harvey shook his head and took a swig of coffee.

Mary caught Michelle's attention and rolled her eyes. She grinned in return and followed Mary over to the sink. "Doc's in good form, he must be feeling a lot better."

"So long as he doesn't overdo it. I'm going to chase Harv out of here in a minute and see if I can get Luke upstairs to bed for a rest."

"On that note I'll get out your hair." She raised her voice. "Take it easy, Doc. I got horses to ride and chores to do. I'll come by tomorrow. See ya, Harvey." She blew Mary a kiss and left.

She might as well stop at Pat's and work Spud and Rain before heading back to the ranch. Coleman rodeo was coming up quick. She'd have to decide if both horses would make the trip or just Spud. Michelle made a mental note to check the website and see if they were offering exhibition runs. Rain wasn't ready to compete yet, but the experience of being at the event and getting used to the strange arena and the crowds would do her good.

It took two hours to work both horses and take care of them. She checked their blankets and fed both one last carrot before putting her tack away. No one else was around so Michelle flicked off the arena lights and then the barn lights as she left the building. The moon was just rising and flooded the prairie with muted silver light. A chill wind wound its way through the hills and nipped at her nose. Gratefully, she climbed into the truck, started it and turned the heat on full. Winter wasn't done with southern Alberta yet, it seemed.

A jack rabbit darted across the gravel road, his coat a mixture of winter white and brindled summer brown. "Stupid critter," she remarked as the animal bolted back out of the ditch in front of the truck. Instead of continuing across the road it ran straight down the centre. She slowed down and waited until the jack finally veered off and disappeared into the moonlit shadows.

"Must be my night for critters," Michelle remarked. A small herd of mule deer bounded across the lane when she rounded the end of the coulee by the ranch gate. The lights were on in the kitchen so Cale must be home already. She parked beside the clinic truck, killed the engine and stepped down from the cab. The yard light illuminated the pens by the barn where the cattle with young calves mooed at her. She started across the gravel to check on them.

"They're all done for the night, Michelle," Cale called from the porch.

She halted and made her way to the house, taking the steps two at time. Cale waited for her in the doorway, a grin on his handsome face and a tea towel slung across one shoulder.

"Busy in the kitchen, my little house husband?"

"Yes, ma'am," he quipped. "How was your busy day at the office?" He wrapped an arm around her shoulder and drew her into the house.

"Busy," she responded and turned her face up for his kiss.

"I like the sound of that *husband*, not the house part of course, but husband sounds pretty good to me. Get down, dog." Cale flapped the tea towel at Crazy Puppy who leaped about like a wild thing to greet them when they entered the kitchen.

"Down, mutt." Michelle slipped out from under Cale's arm and grabbed the dog's collar until he settled down. "Good girl, Storm." She greeted the black dog lying on her bed by the stove.

"Have you been home long? What do you want for supper?" Michelle mentally catalogued what left overs were in the fridge.

"Long enough. Dinner's ready and waiting."

"Thanks, that's great."

"Sit down, I'll get the hamburger helper."

"Ohhh, gourmet!" Michelle teased him.

"Be careful, woman. The chef is very temperamental." Cale waved a serving spoon at her.

"Yes, sir. Warning noted."

Silence fell over the room while they applied themselves to eating. Only the occasional thump of Storm's tail on the floor broke the peace. Michelle pushed her empty plate back and got up. "Coffee?" She raised an eyebrow at her tablemate.

"Please."

She crossed the room to the counter, filled two mugs and brought the coffee back to the table. Setting them down, she scooped up the dirty plates and deposited them in the sink. Back at the table she sank into her chair and rested her elbows on the placemat.

"Tired?" Cale ran a hand over her hair.

"Beat."

"How did the horses go today? That Spud horse ready to go win some cash?"

"They both ran well. I'm thinking of taking Rain down to Crowsnest if there's some exhibition runs available. Spud's full of beans, he turned some really nice barrels tonight."

"When are you planning to leave?"

"Haven't decided yet. The first go isn't until the evening on the Friday. I can't decide if I should haul down early Friday or go Thursday afternoon and let them settle in a bit over night."

"I guess it'll depend on whether you take the mare or not. It wouldn't hurt to let her get used to the place beforehand." Cale rubbed a hand across his face.

"What?" Michelle frowned at him. "What's that look for?" she persisted when he remained silent.

"Nothing, just tired."

"Are you worried about Rob being there?" she guessed.

"In a roundabout way. I'm worried about you and what he might try. Have you talked to Kayla? Is she going down?"

"I think so. She doesn't have a show that weekend and I don't think she's about to let him off his leash just yet."

"Well that makes me feel a bit better."

"I can handle Rob," Michelle protested.

Cale snorted. "Like you handled him the day he broke in here?"

She had the grace to blush. "Okay, I give you that. But he took me by surprise, I won't make that mistake twice, believe me."

"Just try to stay out of his way, okay?"

"That's my plan. Are you going to be able to make it for Friday night? I could use the help, especially if I have both horses running."

"I'd like to, but it depends on the clinic and if Carrie can get here by then."

"Oh, I didn't realize you'd gotten ahold of her. When's she supposed to be coming?"

"Actually, I didn't manage to reach her, but Stacey kept trying until she got her. Carrie said she'd be here this weekend but she wasn't sure if it would be Saturday or Sunday yet."

117

"Stacey's really a big help at the clinic, isn't she?"

"Yeah," Cale's tone was wary. "It frees Mary up to ride herd on Doc and keep him from overdoing it."

"Don't look like that, for heaven's sake." Michelle laughed. "I'm not going to attack the woman. She seems to really like working there. I imagine she gets pretty lonely when George is gone, she's not used to not having people around all the time. It helps you, and it helps Mary and Doc. If she wasn't there, I'd have to try and fit it in."

"She really a good person, Chelly. You'll like her if you just give her a chance."

"I'm working on it. As long as she keeps those pretty little paws off you I'm good." A thought suddenly struck her. "Did you get the eggs when you came home?"

"Damn, no. I did the stock for you and forgot about the chickens."

"You finish your coffee. I'll take the dogs out for a pee and do the chicken girls at the same time." She got up and Storm and her offspring scrambled to their feet. "C'mon, mutts. Let's go for a pee." Grabbing her coat from the back of the chair where she'd left it earlier, Michelle let the dogs out of the kitchen into the mudroom. They milled there while she shoved her feet into boots and pulled on gloves. Crazy Puppy made a flying leap out the door and down the steps when she held it open for him. Storm followed at a more sedate pace.

"Stick around you two. No chasing coyotes." Storm woofed from the shadows by the shed.

The cherry red glow of the heat lamp in the chicken house welcomed her. There was something comforting about the sight on a cold windy night. She ducked through the low doorway and collected the basket from the hook by the door. The hens were settled for the night, some in the straw filled nesting boxes, some huddled in groups on the perches situated around the shed. Without disturbing them, Michelle slipped a hand under the drowsy birds and extracted the warm eggs. After emptying the nests she checked on the floor in corners and the other places she knew certain hens liked to lay their eggs. Her basket full, she inspected the levels of feed and water. Both would do for the night, she made a mental note to clean and refill the waterer in the morning.

"Night, chicken girls." The hens clucked sleepily and settled down again. Michelle slipped out the door and secured it from the outside. Last thing she needed was for the coyotes or fox to get in. "Here, dogs!" She scanned the yard for the two animals. Nearby in the coulee the coyotes yodelled to each other. *Damn, if those stupid mutts are down there chasing coyotes...* "Storm! Puppy!" Crossing the yard with long strides, she set the eggs on the porch step. Turning back, she called the dogs again. When there was no reply, she set off toward the corrals muttering curses and turning her collar up against the north wind. "Storm!"

119

An answering woof came from behind the barn. The dogs came bounding out of the shadows looking very pleased with themselves. Well, actually, Crazy Puppy bounded, Storm came at a more sedate pace.

Michelle's nose wrinkled as they came closer. "Oh, for the love of Pete! You managed to scare up a skunk, you idiots. I should lock you in a stall in the barn for the night." She stalked across the yard to the house, the dogs on her heels. "Cale," she called when she let them into the mud room. "Can you bring the vinegar, the damn dogs got into it with a skunk."

He poked his head in from the kitchen. "Ack, God. Smells like a direct hit. Do you want help?"

She shook her head. "I'll take care of it in the shower out here. Can you drag the dog bed out here for me, though? These two are sleeping out here tonight."

"Here." Cale put the big jug of vinegar down by the door and shut it as quickly as could.

Taking the puppy by the collar she dragged him into the small heated bathroom off the mudroom. Slamming the door shut on him, she went to retrieve the vinegar. Storm blinked at her with big solemn eyes. "You, dog, should know better than to mess with a skunk. What were you thinking?" Storm squeezed into the bathroom with her and sat down leaning against the closed door while Michelle wrestled the younger dog into the shower stall. Dowsing him thoroughly with the white vinegar she tried not to breathe through her nose. Her eyes ran from the mixture of fumes. Crazy Puppy set up a howl of protest which did nothing to improve her mood.

"Will you shut up?" She glared at the dog. He stopped momentarily, and then started up in full voice once more. Ignoring the commotion as best she could, Michelle rinsed him clean and then dowsed him in vinegar again. Finally, declaring him as stink free as he was going to get, she dried him and took him out to the mudroom and put him in a kennel. "Wait here til I'm finished with your momma." Cale had brought out the dog bed she asked for and a micro furnace heater which she turned on and pointed at the door of the kennel. "There, that should keep you from getting icicles in your fur until I'm done."

Returning to the tiny bathroom she repeated the process with Storm who thankfully was much more cooperative than her offspring. In short order Michelle dried her off and told her to stay. She used three large towels to clean up the excess water and tidy the room. There was nothing she could do about the stench that permeated the small space. Like skunk with French fries on the side. She giggled. Wasting no time, she dragged the thick bed into the room where it took up the available floor space. Storm flopped down on it, her head resting on her paws and an apologetic expression in her dark eyes. Michelle ruffled the fur on her head and went to collect the puppy from his kennel prison where he was protesting his incarceration at the top of his lungs.

"You almost done?" Cale stood in the kitchen doorway. "Sounds like you're killing him." He chuckled.

"Almost finished, and right about now I'd be more than happy to kill him."

"I made a fresh pot of coffee." He disappeared back into the other room.

"C'mon, mutt." She gripped the puppy's collar and herded him in with his mother. "You can both stay there until morning. Then we'll see how much you still reek." Michelle closed the door with a decisive snap.

"You stink," Cale greeted her when she stepped into the kitchen.

"Going to shower." She didn't hesitate but carried on down the hall. "Is there anymore vinegar?"

Cale followed her into the downstairs bathroom. "Just this." He held up a small jug of apple cider vinegar.

"Great." She sniffed and took the bottle from his outstretched hand.

He retreated as fast as he could. Shaking her head, she stripped and bundled the clothes into a spare plastic bag from the storage cupboard under the sink. Standing under the spray of hot water she scrubbed until it felt like her skin was raw. She took a deep breath and upended the jug of vinegar over her head. Gagging on the sharp aroma, she tossed the empty jug out of the stall and scrubbed at her hair while trying not to inhale. Sticking her head out the shower curtain she took a desperate breath. The cloying smell of skunk stuck in her throat but it was easier to breathe than the mixed scents of skunk and cider vinegar inside the steamy stall. When she was as clean and odour free as possible she turned off the water and dried off. Wrapping a towel around her dripping hair and a large bath sheet around her body, she gathered up the bag of her clothes and returned to the kitchen.

"You certainly smell better." Cale handed her a mug of coffee. "Here, give me those." He took the bag of clothes and disappeared into the laundry room. He came back with a big house coat. "Put this on and give those towels. They might as well go in the same wash."

"You just want to get me naked," she teased dropping the bath sheet to the floor.

Cale stepped closer and wrapped the robe around her. "You'll catch your death of cold, woman." He kissed her nose. "Interesting perfume you have on. Eau de Fish and Chips with an under note of Pepe le Pew."

"Ha ha, very funny." She took the coffee and sat down in the big arm chair by the stove, tucking her feet up under her.

"Be right back." He waved the wet towel at her and unwrapped the one from her hair on the way by. "I'll bring you back a comb for that rat's nest."

"Gee thanks, you're all heart." Michelle took a huge gulp of coffee and leaned her head on the back of the chair. "Damn, I forgot the stupid eggs on the porch." Untangling herself from the folds of the robe she padded across the floor in her bare feet and slipped out to retrieve the basket of eggs from its perch on the edge of the porch step.

Cale had returned to the kitchen by the time she came back. "Forgot the eggs on the porch." She held the basket up before setting it on the counter by the sink. "I sure don't feel like washing them right now."

"Stick them in the egg fridge and leave them til morning. It's not gonna hurt anything."

"I guess..." Michelle opened the door of the small fridge kept especially for the eggs and made room for the basket. Shutting the door she retrieved her mug of coffee from the floor by the arm chair and curled up in it again. She ran a hand through her tangled hair and then gave up trying to tame it.

"Let me." Cale stood behind her and gently brushed out the snarls.

Her eyes kept closing and her head nodding under his ministrations. He reached down and caught the half full mug when it slipped from her hand. "It's bed time, I think." Setting the brush on the wide back of the chair, he came around to the front and lifted her into his arms.

Michelle snuggled into him and wrapped her arms around his neck. "Mmmm, I could get used to this," she murmured. Cale carried her down the hall and tucked her into the big bed in the front bedroom.

"Be right back, just gonna go turn out the lights."

Michelle didn't hear him come back.

Chapter Nine

With a sigh of relief Michelle pulled into the Coleman Sports Complex. The sun was sinking behind the mountains turning the low lying clouds into a glorious vista of magenta and salmon edged with gold. The eerie sight of the Frank slide which she'd just driven through still sent shivers down her spine. The road snaking through the huge stones looming on either side never failed to give her the willies. She refused to look up at Turtle Mountain which reared its head on the south side of the highway. The thought of all those tons of rock and shale breaking loose and sliding down into the valley burying the small mining town and its inhabitants was just plain terrifying. Even though it happened in 1903 Michelle was always sure she could hear the thunder of the slide and the silent screams of those who lay buried there.

Shaking off the morbid thoughts, she jumped out of the cab and headed to the entry office to pick up her number and get the stabling assignment. In the end she'd decided to only bring Spud. Cale wasn't going to be able to come down for sure and Pat wasn't going to be around to help either. One horse made things so much less complicated.

The brightly lit office made her blink after the gathering darkness outside. Everything was in order and she was back out the door in a matter of minutes. She checked on Spud through the window at his head before getting back in the truck. "Just a few more minutes, bud. Then it's dinner and a nice soft bed for you," she promised him.

The roll up door was open at the back of the building and she parked beside the other trailers pulled up to unload. Leaving the horse in the trailer, she went inside to scope out where her assigned stalls were. They should be side by side, one for the horse and a tack stall. There was a cot and blankets in the storage area of the trailer but she'd booked a room at the hotel in town. It was only minutes away and she could be at the barn quickly if need be. Locating the stalls by the paper with her name on it pinned to the front, she was pleased it was at the end of an aisle and near a man door. It would be relatively quiet for Spud without a lot of competitor traffic going by at all hours. The man door offered her a quick way in and out of the building as well. She poked her head out the door. There was plenty of room to pull the truck and trailer up to the door which would make it so much easier to get all the gear inside. This was when she really wished she had a travelling buddy to help with the slugging.

She located the area where the shavings were stored and commandeered the wheel barrow upturned on the pile. In short order she had the stall ready with a deep bed of sweet smelling shavings. The tack stall only needed a quick sweeping before Michelle went to fetch Spud. He whickered when she opened the rear gate and stepped up into the trailer. "Hey buddy, you ready to get off this thing?" She unclipped the trailer tie, slipped the lead shank off his shoulders, unlatched the divider and secured it to the side of the trailer. Spud followed her willingly, hopping down beside her being careful not to bump her. "Good man." She patted his shoulder. Going around to the storage compartment, she unlocked it and pulled out the water bucket and a feed bin. "Don't worry, I'll come back for the feed." Spud snatched a mouthful of hay from the hay bale by the door before she could stop him. "Give it a rest, you're not that hungry." Michelle smacked him lightly on the shoulder.

It took her the better part of an hour to get him settled, pull the rig around the side of the building by the door at the end of her aisle and drag everything inside. The only things she left in the tack compartment were her saddle, pads, and bridles. She wasn't taking any chances of someone breaking into the locked tack room in the barn and making off with her tack. The trailer was far more secure. It was hard to see in the shadows thrown by the overhead lights in the parking lot. It took longer than usual to unhitch the fifth wheel and get it locked down. She pulled the truck forward and parked it just ahead of the trailer.

"Hey Michelle!" Another competitor greeted her when she re-entered the barn.

"Hey Allie. Who'd you bring?"

"Flint. Looks like I'm your neighbor. We can keep an eye on each other's stuff. Is Pat coming?"

"Great, I was hoping it would be someone I knew. No, Caramel pulled up lame yesterday. Nothing too serious, but she can't run this weekend."

"That sucks. You bring Spud?" Allie peered into the stall.

"Yeah. I left the mare at home this time. One is enough to handle on my own and she's not really ready yet."

"How's your boy running?"

"We've had some good times at home. I guess we'll see tomorrow night how it goes here." Allie shrugged pragmatically.

"You want to go grab a bite? I'm gonna let him settle and eat his dinner before I let him get the kinks out."

"Sure," Allie agreed. "I didn't get a chance to get something on the road. Wanted to beat the weather."

"What weather?"

"There's a snowfall warning for the mountains. It's supposed to start tonight or tomorrow. But it can change, you know that."

"Damn, I didn't have the radio on. I hate driving in a storm." Michelle shuddered. Memories of the wreck just south of Edmonton came rushing back.

"Can't blame you. Not after…well you know," Allie didn't finish the sentence. "We're here safe and sound, let's go get some grub." She grabbed Michelle's arm and towed her toward the door. "I'll drive."

She got in the passenger side and leaned back happy to let someone else drive. "Where do you want to go? Chris' or Popiel's."

"Let's try Chris'. We're early enough it shouldn't be too busy and the food is great." Allie drove out of the parking lot and pointed the truck towards the downtown. A few minutes later she parked in front of the restaurant.

Michelle followed her through the door into the welcome warmth of the building. She waved to couple of cowboys at a table in the corner. Thank God Rob was nowhere in sight.

"Hey, ladies. Nice to see you back in this neck of the woods," Chris greeted them. "Take any table you'd like. Anita will be with you in a minute to get your order. Menus are on the table."

"Allie, over here." Two other barrel racers waved from a table in the corner. "Come join us, there's plenty of room."

Michelle and Allie weaved through the tables in the small room and took the two empty seats. "Good to see you, Joanie. Bonnie." Michelle grinned at her competitors.

"You bring that big Spud horse? If he's runnin' like he can I might as well pack up my girl and head home before it blizzards," Joanie quipped.

"I haven't had him out all winter so I'm not expecting anything special out of him. Just didn't want to miss a chance to get some points." Michelle hung her hat on the back of her chair and smoothed her hair. "That mare of yours has some crazy speed I wouldn't count her out."

The girls ordered and continued to gossip and talk about the other competition during the meal. Finally, Allie drained her beer and looked at Michelle. "You ready to get back? We should be able to use the arena for a bit."

"Works for me. You guys coming?" She glanced at Joanie and Bonnie.

"Not us," they chimed. "We're headed to Pure Country in Blairmore. You sure you don't wanna come? All those cowboys in tight blue jeans...I bet that's where Rob Chetwynd will show up..." Bonnie's eyes sparkled with deviltry.

"He's married," Michelle said and gave the woman a frosty stare.

"Didn't seem to slow him down last time I saw him—Ow!" Bonnie rubbed her shin and glared at Joanie. "What was that for?"

"Really?" Joanie tipped her head toward Michelle.

"Oh...yeah...well..." She had the grace to blush bright red. "He's the one that did the suggesting, I only agreed with him."

"Try saying no next time." Michelle stood up and stalked to the cash register to pay for her meal. Allie joined her.

131

The night air had a sharp edge to it, overhead the wind was whining in the wires and the branches of the evergreens. "Smells like snow." Allie observed as they got in the truck. "I'm surprised it hasn't started yet."

"I'll be happy if it blows itself out by the time I have to drive home." Michelle worried her bottom lip with her teeth.

"Me too."

When they reached the Sports Complex the lot was full of rigs and motorhomes. "Looks like some of the rough stock riders are here already," Allie said.

"Have they posted the draw yet for tomorrow? I need to charge my phone and it won't bring up the webpage." Michelle put her cell away in annoyance.

"I get shitty reception here anyway. They'll have it posted by the event office," Allie said. She found a spot not too far from the doors and parked. "C'mon, let's get in where it's warm."

She dashed across the pavement, Michelle followed, laughing when her friend slipped on a patch of black ice and swore at the top of her lungs.

The moist heat of the barn felt good on her cold cheeks. Spud seemed as eager as she was to stretch his legs. She ducked out the man door at the end of the aisle and brought her tack into the barn. In short order she had the gelding at the entry way to the arena. Allie was right behind her. A few other riders were circling the edges, a few ropers at the far end twirling their ropes

132

overhead. She led Spud through the gate, leaving it open behind her for Allie to close after she came through. Michelle stopped in the middle of the ring and tightened her cinch. Out of habit she checked the fit of the bridle and other equipment before swinging up into the saddle.

The horse jigged under her for a moment before settling down. She let him go forward and chose a path to the inside of the rail. The big gelding was happy to work at a relaxed ground eating trot, his head low and his back nicely rounded. After working at the trot in both directions for a while, Michelle gathered him up a bit and picked up a lope. He shook his head and snorted wanting to increase the pace. She deepened her seat and picked up her rein hand to restrain him. "Soon enough, buddy. Just have some patience." She ran a hand down his neck.

Once the edge had worn off, Michelle slowed him to a walk and let him blow a bit. Allie came up alongside.

"Looks like we'll have the place to ourselves in a minute." Allie indicated the other riders exiting the ring with a wave of her hand.

"I'm almost done anyway, but I think I'll run the pattern a couple of times now there's room. What about you?" Michelle glanced at her friend.

"That was my plan too. You want to go first, or shall I?"

"I'll go, if you don't mind."

"Sure." Allie jogged her mare over to a corner. "You'll just have to pretend there are barrels out here," she joked.

Michelle took Spud down the chute toward the holding area and the gelding became all business. His excitement came clearly through the reins and the big muscles bunching under her. Running her hand down his neck to quiet him, she let him settle for a second before turning her toward the arena. His black tipped ears were rigid and pointed at the bright light of the ring. Leaning forward she gave him the signal he was waiting for. The horse leaped forward and exploded out of the alleyway. Even without the barrels they ran the pattern accurately and fast. Michelle jumped off when she pulled up after the run, unclipped the short rein from one side of the bit and led the blowing horse out to check the path of their footfalls in the soft footing of the ring.

"Good boy." She slapped his shoulder in appreciation. "Any closer and I'll have my knee in a barrel tomorrow night."

"Nice run." Allie jogged Flint up and halted beside her. "You gonna go again?"

Michelle shook her head. "Nope, we're good. He knows his business and that's enough to keep him sharp for tomorrow. You go ahead. Just wait and I'll rake my tracks smooth."

"Thanks." Allie and Flint disappeared into the shadows of the chute.

Michelle wasted no time in raking Spud's tracks out of the dirt. Setting the rake back on the outside of the boards she led the gelding to a corner out of the way. "Okay, you're clear!"

Flint burst into the ring and flew toward the spot where the first barrel would be. She overshot the mark a bit but made a good recovery. Rounding the second barrel they raced for the top marker. Michelle caught her breath when the mare stumbled a bit going into the turn. She managed to stay upright and stretched low as she ran for the finish line.

"Whew, I thought we were gonna have a wreck for a second." Allie and Flint jogged back into the ring. "I don't know what happened, the footing seems good. She just kinda hesitated going in" Allie slid down and checked her horse's legs.

"Are you gonna run it again?" Michelle walked over to them.

"Yeah. She doesn't seem to be any the worse for wear and I don't want to leave it on a bad note." Allie swung back into the saddle. This time she didn't run out of the chute but instead turned the mare and ran the pattern at a fast controlled canter. Flint turned the top barrel position with no hesitation and no stumble.

"That looked better," Michelle called. Spud stood at her shoulder and turned back to him. Flipping the left stirrup over the seat of the saddle she loosened the cinch. "I'm gonna put him away unless you need me."

"I think I'll just do a little flat work with her. I'm fine, and I see a couple of the other girls are coming." Allie nodded toward the gate.

"Okay, see you later, then. I'm at the BCM, where are you staying?"

"Same, I'll catch you later."

Michelle untacked Spud by the stall and threw a cooler over him to keep off the chill til he dried off. By the time she'd lugged her tack back out to the trailer and locked it up tight, the gelding was fairly dry. She used the curry to loosen the dried sweat and then finished with the dandy and body brush. After combing his mane and tail, she wet a small towel and wiped his eyes and nose clean of sweat and arena dust. Using the same cloth, she rinsed it and lifted the gelding's tail aside to wash any dirt and grime from between his buttocks. The fine dust from the arena that got thrown up could irritate the sensitive skin there.

She dug in her pocket and produced a treat. Spud lipped it up and looked for more. "One is all you need. Quit begging." With a practice twist of her arm she threw the blanket over him and secured. Leading him into the stall, she took off his halter and gave him a good scratch under his mane. The gelding shook his head when she was done and lowered his head to the hay in the corner of the stall. After checking the level of the water and re-checking that there was nothing caught in his hooves, Michelle left the stall and slid the door shut. She secured the latch and then slid the halter through the bars and fastened it just for safe measure. The last thing she needed was to go chasing her horse in the middle of the night. The card with her contact info was tacked to the stall, so if, God forbid, something did go wrong they could reach her.

Head down, she turned toward the door at the end of the aisle. "Oh, I'm sorry...Wait, no I'm not!" She glared up at the man she'd just run into. "What the hell are you doing here?" she demanded of Rob Chetwynd. The very last person on earth she wanted to see.

"Just checkin' on you, darlin'." He grinned down at her.

"Like hell. I don't need you checking on me. Move." She went to shove past him.

"Just being neighborly, is all." He caught her arm.

"Piss off before I—"

"Rob? Where'd you get to?" Kayla appeared at the other end of the aisle, the overhead lights casting a halo around her blonde head. "Oh, there you are. Hi, Michelle." She strode across the rubber mats on the floor toward them.

"Hey Kayla. Call off your cowboy, will you?" Michelle looked pointedly at the hand on her arm.

"Rob, you promised." There was steel behind the words.

"Aw, now, honey girl—" Rob let go of Michelle and took a step back.

"Don't you honey girl me, Rob Chetwynd. You've been drinking, I can smell it from here so don't bother to deny it." Kayla stepped past Michelle and grabbed her husband by the arm. "Sorry to bother you, Michelle. If he shows up to harass you again just let me know." She dragged him away.

"C'mon, Kay. Don't be such a hard ass…" Rob's voice faded away.

Shaking her head, Michelle left the barn and got into the truck as huge wet flakes of snow spiraled out of the cloudy sky. "Damn, I wish the truck had an automatic start." She shivered while she waited for the glow plug and then started the engine. Cold air blew out of the vents and she killed the fan until the engine warmed up a bit. "Stupid, stupid snow. Why did it have to pick this weekend to come down like this?" The short drive to the hotel didn't heat the truck much. Michelle parked by the office and went in to collect her key. The place wasn't fancy but it suited her purpose well enough. The room was clean and the shower had good pressure.

There was no point in unpacking the small duffle bag with her things in it. She found the makeup bag and stripped off her clothes on the way to the shower. The hot water was welcome and warmed her up. Dressed in sweats and a t-shirt she left the bathroom door open and stretched out on the bed. *I should call Cale and let him know I got here okay.* The cell phone only showed a bar and a half for reception. There was a pay phone by the front office but the thought of going out in the wind and snow didn't hold much appeal. She settled for sending a text, once the weather cleared maybe it would go through. She should let him know Rob was here before someone else told him. All the gossips in the world should just go jump in a hole and pull it in after them.

Idly, she flicked on the TV and channel surfed. There wasn't much worth watching except some reruns of current sitcoms. That amused her for about an hour. Maybe she should get dressed and go to the bar. That was probably where Allie was. The wind rattling the window pane and snow pelting the glass made that option less than desirable. Instead, she snuggled under the comforter and picked up the book she'd left on the bedside table before her shower. When her vision started to blur she put the book down and turned out the lights. *Hope Spud is getting a good rest. Man, I miss Cale.*

Chapter Ten

Snow was still falling when Michelle got out of bed and pulled back the drapes in the morning. A blanket of white obscured the mountains and visibility was restricted to a few feet. At least Spud was safe at the barns. She didn't have to worry about hauling him anywhere in this mess. A glance in the mirror over the dresser told her she shouldn't have gone to bed with wet hair last night. It was only seven-thirty, plenty of time to shower and get something to eat before going to feed Spud and clean his stall. The girls in the slack were running at the end of the other events that started at ten. Maybe she'd shower and then go take care of Spud before getting breakfast.

Putting thought to action she took the time to blow dry her hair before putting on her outer gear and driving to the rodeo barn. She shook the snow from her hat and shoulders inside the door and stomped the muck from her boots. The barn was already bustling with other competitors and the stock contractors hanging around the concession or taking care of their animals. She grinned, no sign of the rough stock riders. They'd be sleeping off last night's revelry. Only the bull doggers and tie down ropers had horses to care for, the others

140

travelled light with just their rigging bag and some extra clothes.

Spud whinnied as he recognized her footsteps when she neared his stall. "Okay, I'm coming," she called to him. Unlocking the chain on the tack stall, she collected his hay and went to open his stall and drop it in. The water in his bucket was half gone so she filled it before going to get his grain. Setting the rubber tub in the corner, she moved the gelding over so she could clean the stall around him. Thankfully, he was a neat horse. All the manure was in one corner at the back and only a spot in the centre of the stall was dark with urine. She skipped it out and into the waiting wheelbarrow in record time. The manure dump was by the shavings pit. Stalls had to be cleaned and the waste in the dump by nine or there'd be penalties. The complex staff would remove it with the tractor before anyone from the public would show up.

Tipping her contribution into the pile, Michelle returned the wheelbarrow and fork to the tack room. "Mornin', Allie." She met the other girl coming down the aisle when she stepped out of the stall door.

"Mornin'. You missed a good party last night." Allie yawned. "But, man, I'm feeling it this morning."

"I thought about going down to the hotel but the idea of going out in the snow kind of talked me out of it."

"You done already?" Allie waved at Spud's stall.

"Just finished. I'm headed down to Chris' for some breakfast."

"If I don't take too long I'll see you there. Otherwise I'll have to make do with the concession."

"I'm off, but I'll save you a seat." Michelle waved and after one last check to be sure Spud had everything he needed, she left the building.

Chris' place was jammed on a Friday morning so she tried Popeil's. There was an empty table available, she sat down and ordered coffee and breakfast. A couple of girls she knew joined her and the meal passed quickly. Allie showed up just as Michelle got a coffee refill. The two girls she'd shared breakfast with left and Allie dropped into one of the vacated chairs.

"Man, Chris' is insane! I couldn't get in and I didn't see you anywhere so I thought I'd try here. You done already?" She paused to give the waitress her order.

"Just having another cup of coffee." She glanced at her watch. "Where are they with the slack?"

"Tie down roping is done and they've started on the bull dogging. They won't be done before we get back if you want to keep me company while I eat."

"Sure. I want to watch some of the girls in the slack, there's a few up and comers there on some good horses." Michelle leaned back and people watched out the front window while Allie inhaled her food. Even bundled up against the weather the diversity of people in a small town like Coleman never ceased to amaze her.

"Ready?"

Allie startled Michelle out of her contemplation of the locals parading by on the sidewalk outside. She scrambled to her feet and drained the last of her coffee. "Sure, let's go. You drive down or do you need a ride?"

I caught a ride down, so if you don't mind, a lift would be great."

"No problem." She shrugged into her jacket and fished the keys out of her pocket. The wind whipped snow stung her face when they stepped out of the restaurant. Hunching her shoulders Michelle ran for the shelter of the truck. Inside the cab it seemed strangely quiet after the howling storm outside. "Damn, I hope this eases off before I have to drive home."

"You and me both," Allie agreed.

The short drive back to the rodeo grounds took longer than usual. A few cars fishtailed in front of them and a rear wheel drive pickup ended up facing the wrong way on the sidewalk. Weaving her way carefully through the carnage, she heaved a sigh of relief when she pulled up in the lee of the sportsplex building. Rather than leave the tack in the trailer Michelle decided to bring it in and let the leather warm up. If the storm got worse like it threatened to, she didn't want to be fumbling around in the cold and dark later. Allie held the half door to keep the wind from slamming it closed while Michelle gathered her gear. Locking the storage area, the two girls battled their way to the entrance.

"Thanks for the help." Michelle set the saddle on its nose and draped the bridle and pad over the upturned end. She unlocked the tack stall and stored her equipment. After checking on Spud and Flint the women headed for the arena where a sparse crowd was cheering on the girls racing in the slack. "Remember those days?" She grinned at Allie. "I thought I'd never make it into the evening performance."

"Me too. No early morning hauling and hanging around."

They climbed the bleacher like seats and found a good vantage point. They spent the next hour or so watching the competitors and comparing notes on the riders and their horses. "You staying to watch the team roping?" Allie stood up and stretched.

"Nope. I'm gonna go brush Spud and take a peek and see if that little arena is free to give him a bit of a workout before tonight. If it wasn't for the stupid snow I'd take him for a bit of a ride up into the trees."

Allie laughed. "Good luck with that in this weather. I think I'm gonna stick around, see who shows up." She sat back down.

"Hoping to run into Clay, or his big brother?" Michelle teased.

"Maybe, maybe not." She grinned back.

Michelle left the stands while they were setting up for the team roping slack. After brushing the gelding and giving him a light workout to loosen his muscles, she drove back to the hotel. On the way she picked up a large coffee and some snacks. Pulling up outside the hotel room, she let herself in and tossed the truck keys on the dresser by the TV. Stretched out on the bed she propped herself up with pillows and flipped through the channels while enjoying her coffee. Crumpling the chip bag in her hand she tossed it in the general direction of the garbage can.

A glance at the clock told her it was only two-thirty. Time for a nap before she needed to get ready for the evening go. Turning on her side, she punched the remote to turn off the TV and rearranged the pillows to get comfortable. It was nice to be warm and cozy while the wind howled outside.

It was getting dark when she woke up. Turning on the bedside lamp she checked her phone for the time. Four o'clock. Time to get moving. She pulled her good shirt out of the duffle bag along with a pair of clean jeans. It only took a moment to transfer her belt with the big championship buckle from her dirty jeans to the new ones. Tucking the flashy shirt into the waist band she settled the pants on her hips and did up the belt. Hair had escaped from her braid so she spent a few minutes brushing it out and re-braiding it. She shrugged into her jacket and picked her hat up from the chair where she'd tossed it. It was still a bit damp from the snow, but hopefully Spud would be moving so fast nobody would notice. She grinned.

The parking lot was filling up fast when she got to the sportsplex. It was going to be a good crowd in spite of the storm. Excitement curled in her gut and adrenalin made her skin crawl. No more coffee or she'd be so hyped it would affect Spud's performance. Michelle left the truck and entered the building. She circled the barn area a few times to try and wear off some of the pre-run nervous energy. The house lights were up and the chute area was lined with competitors perched on the top rail. Saddle Bronc was the first event, the stock contractors were busy getting the horses sorted so they'd load into the chutes in the right order of go. The draw for mounts had taken place much earlier and the cowboys were comparing their books on the animal's habits and idiosyncrasies.

The big arena clock read six-fifteen. If she wanted to use the practice ring and warm Spud up some she'd have to get a move on. The other girls were starting to show up and there was a general confusion as they all worked to get ready and into the ring. Michelle let Spud move with a low ground-covering trot. The gelding knew his business, there was no point doing any fast work or running any barrels at speed like some of the girls were. When there was a lull, she took her turn and loped Spud through the cloverleaf pattern taking care to be sure where his footfalls were. Satisfied, she pulled him up and stood quietly out of the way. A roar from the main ring accompanied each bronc and rider as they exploded out of the chute. Bare Back followed the Saddle Broncs. Michelle took Spud back to the stall and wandered back to watch the bulls.

She spotted Kayla in the front row of the stands. Her hands clenched on the rail and her face paper white. Rob was third in the go and he'd drawn a bull called Show Down. Michelle hopped up on the chute beside Rolly and punched him in the arm. "Hey, long time no see. What are you doing here?"

"Hey, Chelly. Just came down to see what's what and maybe scare up an outrider or two."

"What happened to your regular guys?"

"Chance took a spill in practice and busted an arm, and to make things worse, Jake had a wreck with some of the youngsters. Busted up the old wagon I use for training and broke his arm and a leg."

"Shitty luck. Doc told me about the arm, didn't know about the leg. You finding anyone to replace them?"

"Not so far. Some of the guys will loan me some of their outriders, but if we're in the same heat or we're running back to back, it gets kinda hard."

"Oh, here we go." She pointed to the chutes as a big Brahma trotted into place and stood tossing his head while the bull rider and his helpers fussed with the bull rope.

"It's exciting to watch, but those boys need their heads read." Michelle shook her head.

"I'll take my chances on the seat of my wagon any day," Rolly agreed.

She stayed to watch Rob, who made the buzzer and scrambled for the chutes when the bull attempted to escape the bull fighters dressed as clowns who hazed it toward the exit. "Gotta go. Wish me luck, I can use the points, not to mention the day money."

She jumped down and headed back to the barns. There was still tie down roping and bull dogging to run yet. This was the worst part, the waiting and itching to just get out there and go for it. Nerves always got the best of her and she made the obligatory trip to the bathroom. Even if she didn't really have to go, she always *thought* she did. Better to be safe than sorry. Before she left the brightly lit room she checked her appearance. Hair still braided, lipstick still in place, shirt tucked in, hat pulled down low. Good to go.

Finally the team ropers returned to the barn area and the bull dogging was under way. She collected Spud, tightened his cinch and checked the tack one more time. She swung up into the saddle and made her way to the practice ring. A couple of turns at the lope and she joined the other women in the holding area. They were fourth to go. No too bad, the arena wouldn't be too torn up by then and she'd have a chance to see how the competitors in front of her handled the footing. She forced herself to breathe deeply and relax.

Spud shifted under her in anticipation. Michelle ran a hand down his neck to soothe him. "Soon, buddy. Soon." The first horse and rider blew down the chute. She craned her neck and stood in the stirrups in order to see as much of the run as she could. They turned in a time of 14.632. She settled back into the saddle with a smile. If Spud ran like she knew he could, they'd beat that time easy. Wheeling the gelding around, she guided him around the small holding pen a few times. The guy manning the gate called to let her know she was on deck. Michelle nodded and waited for the last competitor to come down the chute and pull up. Her eyes were glued to the end of the entry gate anticipating the signal they were ready in the arena. Spud snorted and shook his head, fighting the bridle at bit in his eagerness to run.

"You're up!"

Michelle leaned forward and gave Spud his cue. The gelding exploded beneath her, the crowd's roar seemed a long way away as they rounded the first barrel. She stayed as quiet in the saddle as possible and let him find his path to the second barrel. Down the long straight away to the top, he dipped his shoulder a little lower than she would have liked coming in, but the barrel stayed upright as they brushed by. One last dash to the finish line, Spud stretched out long and low with his ground eating stride, then they flashed out of the ring and down the chute. She pulled the horse up and slapped his neck in appreciation.

"Nice run, Michelle," Allie congratulated her. "I'm gonna have to run my ass off to beat that time."

Michelle glanced at the time posted—13.514. "Good job, Spud man." She let her horse walk a bit to let his breathing slow and his heartrate to return to normal. Once they were clear and had a bit of room, Michelle swung down and loosened the girth. Back at the stall she stripped him down and took him to the wash stall. Rinsing the sweat and arena dirt from him only took a few minutes. Throwing the lead shank over his neck, she covered him with a wool cooler and walked him back to the stall. A roar from the crowd told her that someone had turned in a really good time. She tossed Spud some hay and left him to dry while she went back to watch the rest of the girls run.

At the end of the night, her time still stood. Thank God for that, the day money would help cover her costs. The snow was still coming down thick and fast outside. Hopefully it would be done by the time she had to haul home tomorrow. She made her way back to Spud's stall and removed the damp cooler. Underneath the horse's coat was warm and dry. Soon he was snug and warm in his stable blanket while she rubbed his legs down with liniment, the sharp smell stinging her nose and eyes.

She stood up and stretched. Part of her wanted to join her friends and celebrate at the bar and part of her just wanted to fall into bed. *Damn, I miss Cale.* Pulling her phone out of her pocket she texted him her good news. There was no immediate response and she tried not to be disappointed. By the time the tack was stowed in the trailer and Spud was set for the night, Michelle vetoed the partying and drove to the hotel.

Her phone buzzed while she wrestled with the key in the door. *Maybe it's Cale.* She dropped her coat on the chair and kicked off her boots. Fishing the cell out of a back pocket she called up the message. *Damn!* It was Rob, wanting to know where she was and why wasn't she celebrating. Seemed Rob had high score in the bulls. She texted back, refusing his offer to buy her a beer and neglecting to say where she was at the moment. *Let Kayla ride herd on him.* There was still no message from Cale.

Michelle tried to call Mary but the connection wouldn't go through. *Stupid snow.* Reception in the mountains was always chancy anyway, but why couldn't it just this once give her a break. Giving up on the phone, she turned on the TV. The weather report said the snow should ease up overnight and clear out by midday. Thank goodness for small mercies. Flicking off the news, she wandered into the bathroom and stood under the hot shower. Bed and sleep were high on her list of priorities. She tied her wet hair back in a ponytail and slid between the covers. Almost before her head hit the pillow she was asleep.

* * *

151

Her inner alarm woke her up before the sun. Slipping out of bed she padded to the window and peered out. A few desultory flakes were still falling, but for the most part the snow seemed to have stopped. Good, the drive home shouldn't be too bad. Quickly, she dressed and packed up her few belongings. The hotel office had her credit card so she left the key on the dresser and threw her things into the truck. At the Petro Can she grabbed a large coffee and filled up the tank of the truck. The Saturday slack competitors were milling around the barns, but not too many others were present. Spud whinnied at the sound of her feet when she turned into his aisle. She gave him his breakfast and packed up the contents of the tack stall. By the time everything was loaded in the trailer Spud was done with his grain and looking for his hay.

"You can eat in the trailer, bud." Michelle removed the water bucket, dumped it down the drain at the end of the aisle and retrieved the rubber feed tub from the stall. She stashed them in the storage compartment of the fifth wheel and hurried back to collect Spud.

"C'mon, boy. Let's hit the road. I want to get back home and see Cale."

"You leavin' already?" Allie appeared outside the stall.

"Yeah, I need to get home. You stickin' around?"

"For a while anyway. You planning on going to Drayton in a couple of weeks?"

"I'm entered. Not sure if I'm taking Rain or not, but Spud and me will be there. Don't party too hard." She grinned.

"Don't you worry about me." Allie laughed. "See ya in Drayton."

"Bye." Michelle led Spud out of the stall and through the barn door. The gelding loaded willingly into the trailer and she secured the divider and the back gate. It would be good to get home and see Cale. She loved rodeo but going down the road almost every weekend without Cale was going to suck big time. *At least the snow has stopped.* She maneuvered out of the parking lot and turned onto the main road. Heading east along the Crowsnest highway she contemplated not taking the more direct route of highway 22 north and continuing east to the number 2. Driving through the mountains in April could be tricky, but it was the quickest route home. The road report said the route should be clear. Making her decision Michelle indicated and turned north. The road climbed and followed the narrow valley. The Chain Lakes were strung out along the left hand side of the highway surrounded by snow encrusted evergreens.

The road climbed at bit and at the higher elevation snow covered the asphalt. The truck's four wheel drive engaged and Michelle's stomach clenched. "God, I hate snow." She ground her teeth. Memory flashes of the wreck two years ago set her hands shaking. *It's not going to happen again, it's not going to happen again.* She repeated the mantra over and over. "Quit being stupid. Concentrate on driving. It's not that far," Michelle chastised herself.

A few more miles and the weak sun disappeared behind a bank of thick clouds. Forcing her fingers to relax on the wheel, she kept going. There wasn't any other choice anyway, there was nothing around but mountains, the lakes and the snow covered road. Snow began to fall when she reached the junction of secondary highway 520. *Damn and double damn.* She turned up the radio, the connection to the world outside the cab of the truck in some strange way gave her a sense of safety. Like nothing bad could happen while Ian Tyson was singing about summer wages. It was a silly notion, but it did provide a measure of comfort.

The storm continued to thicken. Michelle spared a second to glare at the radio as the announcer blithely announced the sun was shining in Calgary, and it was overcast in Okotoks and Banff. "Really? What about it's snowing like a bitch south of Longview?" Her attention returned to the road, concentrating on keeping the vehicle straight. Thank God the road was fairly straight. The windshield wipers fought to keep up with the slushy spring snowfall.

A truck passed going in the opposite direction throwing up a veil of slush and snow. The wheels of the pickup caught in the thick wet snow and pulled it toward the shoulder of the road. Michelle fought the wheel, struggling to pull free of the unplowed snow. The trailer fishtailed a bit. Sweat broke out on her forehead and heat swept over her body. In slow motion the truck continued to slide toward the ditch.

"No, no, no, no." Somewhere, someone was chanting and Michelle wished they'd just shut up. Biting her lip, she realized it was her voice. She breathed a sigh of relief when the front wheels caught some traction on a bare bit of road. To her horror, the trailer continued to push forward and shove the pickup deeper into the snow. Her heart stuttered and she swallowed bile as the trailer tilted sideways and slid into the ditch dragging the truck with it. It came to rest half on its side before toppling the rest of the way over.

The seatbelt dug into her neck and shoulder. She killed the engine and fought down the panic. Frantically, she wrestled with the seatbelt and finally managed to get free of it. Bracing her feet against the centre console she forced the driver door open and scrambled out. She landed knee deep in snow and floundered for a moment. *Spud, I have to get to Spud.* Stumbling through the snow Michelle managed to reach the trailer. "Spud? Spud?" Her voice broke and she had to pause and control her panicked breathing. She climbed up the trailer and looked inside. Spud was lying on his side but didn't seem to be in too much distress. Slithering down, Michelle struggled around to the read and forced her cold fingers to undo the latches. The trailer was lying so that the door flopped open unto the drifted snow. Thank God it hadn't landed on the other side, she would have had to prop the damn thing open with something. The gelding nickered when she crawled inside and put a hand on his shoulder. "I know, bud. I'm gonna get you outta here. Just let me think for a minute." Careful to stay clear of his hooves, she checked him over as best she could. He didn't seem to be bleeding and other than being in an awkward position, he didn't seem too distressed. Nothing looked like it was broken.

"Hey! Anybody here? Do you need help?" A man's face appeared in the open trailer door.

"Man, am I glad to see you. Do you have a CB or a phone? I lost mine somewhere." Michelle wriggled backward and out the door. "I need a tow truck and I need to call…"

"I already called the RCMP and you're in luck 'cause I'm the tow truck. I was on my way home from a call when I saw you. Is the horse okay? How many are in there?" He peered into the trailer.

"Just one, and he seems to be okay, but we have to get him out of there." Tears froze on her lashes.

He handed her his cell. "Here, do you want to call someone?"

She took it in trembling fingers. "Thanks." It took two tries to hit the right numbers. Michelle held the phone to her ear and prayed.

156

"Cale? Cale, I'm…" Emotion clogged her throat and she couldn't squeeze the words out.

"Michelle? Where are you? What's wrong?" His voice steadied her nerves and she managed to speak.

"I'm not too far south of Longview on 22. I'm in the ditch and Spud's still on the trailer." Her voice broke.

"Is he hurt? Calm down, Chelly and think. I'm on my way but I need to know what to bring. Does anything look broken? Is there blood?"

"No, no. Nothing looks broken and I can't see any blood."

"Okay, I'll call the RCMP and a tow truck—"

"No, wait." She handed the phone to the tow truck driver. "Can you tell him exactly where we are and that you've already called the RCMP, and you have a tow truck."

She shoved her hands in the pockets of her jacket and shivered. *Spud must be getting cold by now. I should crawl back in and check on him.* Michelle moved toward the trailer. A hand on her shoulder stopped her.

"Michelle, it's Michelle, right? Why don't you get up in my truck and keep warm. You're in shock and standing out here in the snow isn't going to help. You've got a big bump on your head."

"No, I need to stay with him. I can't leave him." She rubbed her forehead, a headache blurred her vision. She sat down involuntarily in a drift. "I'll just sit here and keep him company."

Flashing lights and the wail of a siren caught her attention. Her head was leaning on the truck window and a blanket was wrapped around her. "What the hell?" Michelle tried to sit up but the pain in her head blinded her. "Son of a bitch."

The opposite door opened and let in a blast of cold air. "Michelle. It's me. Just sit still. There's an ambulance on the way." Cale leaned over the driver's seat and pulled the blanket further up her shoulders. He kissed her cheek. She squinted at his blurred features.

"Cale? Spud!" She struggled to push the restricting cover away and fumbled for the door handle. "Spud, I have to get him out of the trailer. He's been in there way too long…"

"Michelle." Cale's hands restrained her. "Michelle, he's fine. We got him out. Doc's here with Pat's rig and we've got him loaded up already. Doc's gonna take him to the clinic and give him a thorough exam."

"I need to go with him. He'll be scared."

"You need to sit still and wait for the EMS guys to get here."

"I don't need an ambulance. I'm fine."

"Don't be stubborn. You need to get your head checked out."

"I'm fine. Let me out." She pushed at him, cursing herself for her weakness.

"Thank God." Cale disappeared and a strange man opened her door.

"Who are you?" Michelle was annoyed the words came out slurred. *Shit, they'll think I've been drinking.*

"Hi, Michelle. I'm John. We're just gonna get you out of here and into the ambulance to check you out. Can you help me a bit? Just put your arms around my shoulders and I'll lift you down."

"I'm fine. Don't need to be checked out." Her head fell forward against the man's shoulder.

"Of course you are. But humour me, okay. It's my job and I don't want to get fired."

"Sure, okay." Michelle let herself be eased down out of the high cab of the tow truck.

When she opened her eyes she was flat on her back. Her stomach wasn't thrilled with the swaying of the vehicle and she gagged.

"Awake are we?" The man beside her laid a hand on her arm. "Just lie still."

"I'm gonna be sick," she managed to get out before her body rebelled entirely. To her embarrassment she choked and vomit came out her nose. *Gross!*

The man, what was his name? Joe, no, John. John raised the head of the bed a bit but kept her spine straight and told her to try not to move too much. He wiped her face and did something to clear her breathing passages. She must have drifted off because the next thing she knew the stretcher was being wheeled down a long corridor. The lights flashing by overhead

159

increased the pain in her head and she closed her eyes.

"My horse, where's my horse?" Michelle fought her way out of the fog clouding her thoughts.

"Your horse is fine, dear. Your husband said you'd be worried about him and to tell you that Doc took him home. Once we get you settled and the doctor has a look at you your husband can come and see you." A white coated woman with a clipboard leaned over her briefly and then hurried off.

The ambulance attendants parked her in a curtained alcove and dimmed the lights. She remembered to thank them before they left. After answering what seemed like a hundred stupid questions, the doctor let Cale in to see her. Her head was feeling much better and her vision was no longer producing double images of everything.

"When can I get out of here?"

"After the doctors take a look at the test results and the x-rays." Cale took her hand and leaned over to kiss her forehead. "You gave me quite a scare. Why didn't you wait until the snow stopped before driving home?"

"It wasn't snowing when I left and the stupid road report said it was clear all the way to Calgary. How's Spud? Did he get hurt? How did you get him out of the trailer? If he's hurt it's all my fault."

One question at a time. He seems fine. Nothing broken for sure. The tow truck winched the trailer upright enough that Spud could walk off. Doc followed me with Pat's rig so we loaded him straight away and Doc took him to the clinic. Don't worry, you know he's in good hands." He paused and ran his hand through his hair. "Christ Michelle, you scared the crap out of me. Do you know how lucky it was that tow truck just happened to come along when he did?"

"I couldn't find my cell. It must have dropped out of my pocket or something...I knew you'd come if I could just get a hold of you." She scrubbed at the tears that sprang to her eyes. "Damn it, I don't know why I'm crying. I hate crying."

"I'll always be there, Michelle. Come hell or high water, woman, all you have to do is holler and I'll be there."

"I know..." She dissolved in tears. "I don't know why I'm crying," she repeated.

"Close your eyes and try to rest. I'll be right here." Cale smoothed the hair back from her face.

A short time later the doctor reappeared. "Well, the good news is you haven't broken anything. You've got a slight concussion, but as long as you've got someone to stay with you I'm inclined to let you go home." He raised a hand when she tried to get up. "On the condition you take it easy and rest. If there's any change, any sudden increase in pain, or change in vision, you get yourself back here on the double. Deal?"

161

"Deal."

"I'll go do the paperwork. The nurse will come and remove the IV and then you can get dressed. Your clothes are under the stretcher."

"Thanks," Cale said and shook the man's hand.

"You're very welcome."

Michelle fidgeted until the nurse arrived and removed the catheter in her arm. It was more than annoying that Cale had to help her get dressed. She couldn't seem to quit crying, which irritated her even more.

"It's just the shock, Chelly. Quit worrying about it."

"I feel like an idiot," she complained.

The nurse returned with the discharge papers. "All set. You just need to sign here and you're free to go."

She scribbled her name and against her better judgement let Cale push her in a wheelchair as far as the door. "I'm not an invalid for heaven's sake."

"Enjoy the pampering while you can," Cale teased her. "Wait here while I go bring the truck around." He loped off in the direction of the parking garage.

The wind was cold so she pulled up the collar of her jacket and huddled deeper into it. Her knees knocked together with the shivers that rolled over her. It seemed to take forever before Cale stopped the truck beside her and hurried around to open the passenger door.

"Sorry, there was a line up to pay. You must be frozen." He scooped her up and deposited her on the truck seat. "I put the seat warmer on so you should be toasty soon."

Michelle leaned her head against the back of the seat. At least they'd only taken her to the hospital in Black Diamond. She didn't think she could have handled the drive from Calgary. If she never saw the inside of Foothills again it would be too soon.

Cale closed her door and went around and got behind the wheel. "Close your eyes if you want. I'll have you home in no time."

"Can we stop and see Spud? I need to see him, make sure he's okay." Her jaw clenched as fresh shivers shook her.

"Spud is fine. I'm taking you straight home. If you want you can call Doc and let him reassure you. That old man could never lie to you." Cale handed her his phone.

She speed dialed Doc and waited for him to pick up. "Doc, it's me."

"Chelly, are you okay. Where are you?"

"I'm with Cale. We're just leaving Black Diamond. How's Spud? Is he okay? Cale won't take me to the clinic, he says we're going right home."

"The horse is fine, he's resting. That boy's right, you need to go home and rest. Come and see your horse in the morning if you're feeling up to it. I'm taking good care of him, you know that."

"But he's okay, right? You're not hiding anything?"

"He's fine. Any bumps he's got are a long way from his heart," Doc assured.

"Okay, thanks. Give him a carrot for me and tell him I'll see him in the morning. Oh, can you let Pat know we're all okay and thank her for loaning her rig?"

"Already done. Pat's here fussing over that horse of yours. See you tomorrow. Love you Chelly Belly."

"I love you too, Doc." She broke the connection and handed the phone back to Cale.

"Feel better?" He reached over and squeezed her hand.

"Yeah. Let's go home."

Chapter Eleven

It was actually three days later before Michelle felt well enough to drive in to the clinic. She felt like a fraud sitting in the passenger seat and letting Cale chauffer her. He parked behind the building and helped her out of the truck.

"I won't break, you know," Michelle tried to keep the annoyance out of her voice.

"Humour me," Cale replied and caught her elbow when she stumbled.

"Fine," she hissed under her breath. "Shit, I hate being useless."

"You're not useless. Quit bitching."

Doc met her in the meds room. "Here sit down for a minute. I need to talk to you." He looked over her head at Cale.

Warning flags went off in her head. "What's wrong? What didn't you tell me?" She tried to stand up but Cale's hand on her shoulder held her still.

"Sit still and let the man talk," he warned.

"Where's Spud? He's not..." She couldn't bring herself to say the word.

"Lord no, Chelly. The horse isn't dead. Do you honestly think I'd keep something like that from you?"

"I guess not." She quit struggling to get up. "So, what's wrong?"

"Considering what he went through the horse is in pretty good shape. But," he held up a hand, "there is a problem. There's an injury to the left hock. I've taken plates and nothing seems broken, but there is considerable soft tissue injury. When he came off the trailer in the ditch the snow was pretty deep and it was getting dark. He seemed to be moving okay and not in any danger. It wasn't until we got back to the clinic and unloaded him that the lameness became apparent."

"You should have told me!"

"What good would that have done? You couldn't do anything we weren't already taking care of. You needed to rest and not be hovering over my shoulder making yourself sick. Be mad at me all you want, Chelly. I'd make the same decision again."

"Okay, okay. How bad is it? How long will he be laid up?"

Cale's hand tightened on her shoulder and Doc refused to meet her gaze. She swallowed hard and waited for the worst.

"The good news is it will heal. With time."

"How long?"

"It's hard to predict with a soft tissue injury. There's still a lot of swelling and it makes it hard to determine what might be underlying problems. Once the edema goes down I'll take more plates."

"How much is all this going to cost? Don't get me wrong, give him whatever he needs, but I need to figure out how to pay for it."

"Don't worry about that right now. I'm going to do shock wave therapy on him and laser his tendons and ligaments starting in a few days. Right now we've got him on some anti-inflammatory drugs, something for pain, and stall rest. We're icing the leg and we've deep bedded him. So quit worrying."

"Can I see him?"

"Of course. You know the way, he's in the stall at the end where it's quieter."

* * *

Michelle was quiet on the way back to the ranch. *How am I going to pay for everything? I know Cale will insist on helping but he's not rolling in dough either. Shit, I haven't even asked about my truck and the trailer yet.* "Cale, how much damage was there to the truck and trailer? I can't believe I forgot about that until right this minute."

"The trailer took the worst of it. The hitch coupling got twisted and there's some good dings in the sides. The truck got off easier, just needs a new tailgate and some body work. I had them towed to Harry's, I figured that's what you'd want."

"Shit, shit. I guess I need to call the insurance company."

"I already talked to Mel. He started the paperwork for you, just needs you to drop in and sign them. Do you want to stop on the way out of town?"

"No, not really. But I guess I should. Do you mind?"

"Of course not." Cale turned the truck around and headed to the insurance broker's office.

It only took a minute to go in, take care of the paperwork and assure Mel she was fine. Hurrying back out to the truck she just wanted to get home and away from town where it seemed everyone on the street wanted to stop and talk, asking how she was, how the horse was. Tension stiffened her neck and increased the pounding in her temples.

"How come you're not at work?" The thought suddenly occurred to Michelle.

"Doc and Carrie are taking care of it until you're back on your feet. Don't worry about it."

"Carrie's here? I didn't know she'd started yet."

"Got here last weekend. By the way, congrats on winning at Coleman. Your cheque's in the mail."

"Really? I knew I won day money. You mean we won the whole deal?"

"Emma called on Sunday night. Your time stood up, so yeah, you've got day money coming as well as the jackpot. Sorry, I clean forgot to tell you."

"Not like you haven't had other things on your mind. At least that'll help with some of the bills."

"Don't worry about the money, Michelle. Doc isn't charging for his services, neither am I, no hospital fees for Spud. But some of the meds are expensive even at cost, and the shock wave is pricey too. If things don't clear up the way they should Doc has talked to Moore's up by Calgary about getting him in for an MRI. We'll manage, Chelly. The important thing is you're okay and Spud is doing good."

"I know. I just can't help worrying. Cattle prices suck right now, I can't even sell some of the heifers to generate some quick cash."

Cale cleared his throat. "George was pretty upset over you getting hurt. He's been calling every day, the first day he called just about every hour on the hour. Stacey convinced him not to come to the hospital or over to the house in case it just upset you. You should give him a call when you feel up to it."

"Yeah, you're right. He makes me mad enough to spit nails but if something happened to him I'd be devastated. I'll call him when I get home. Maybe after I lay down for a bit. My head is about to split open."

Storm and Crazy Puppy met her at the door. She bent down carefully and ruffled their heads. The dogs left with Cale when he went out to do chores. Michelle shuffled down the hall and gratefully sank onto the bed. *Go away headache*. It was hard to think when her hair hurt. She'd had hangovers that hurt less. She would call her brother once she got up. Having decided that, she pushed it to the back of her mind and mulled over how to pay for Spud's medical bills. Rain was still over at Pat's too. She might as well bring her home. The doctor at the hospital insisted she shouldn't exert herself for a week at least. Cale had already made an appointment with Doctor Lewen for her and the hospital was forwarding her reports.

Rolly. What did Rolly say when I talked to him at Coleman? Outriders...he needed outriders. He had a good outfit and was always in the top of the standings in the World Professional Chuckwagon Association. If she remembered right, the outriders got paid by the race and then usually a bonus if the outfit had a good meet. *If I can pick up some rides for the other drivers if they're short...It just might work. I've got Rolly's number somewhere. I wonder if my phone has showed up? Gotta ask Cale.* She drifted off into a fitful slumber before she found the energy to get up.

A barking dog startled Michelle awake. She was only too glad to escape the dream where she waded through snow drifts that got progressively deeper the farther she went. "Storm?" A flailing arm connected with the bedside lamp which crashed to the floor. She lay for a moment attempting to gather her senses.

"Michelle, are you okay?" Cale burst into the room and skidded to a stop. "What happened?"

Just clumsy. I thought I heard Storm barking." She wriggled into an upright position.

"She was. Your brother's here."

170

"Hey, Chelly." George stuck his head in the door. "Should I throw my hat in first?" He grinned referring to Grampa's habit of tossing his hat in the door first if he and Gramma were feuding. If the hat came flying back out he'd hightail it for the barn.

"Come on in, you idiot." She waved a hand and let it fall back to the quilt.

"Look, I'm sorry—" they both spoke at once.

"I'll leave you two to work this out. Yell if you need anything." Cale picked up the lamp and left the room.

"I'll go first," George insisted. "Stacey tore a piece off me about how I behave when I come home. According to her, I'm insensitive and arrogant and a royal pain in the ass."

"She's got that right." Michelle broke in.

"Let me finish. I should have realized how hard it was to take care of everything on your own, especially in the winter. And I should have talked to you before I invited a stranger to live in the house. I just didn't think it would be a problem."

Michelle snorted but held her peace.

"I know, I know. Stacey read me chapter and verse on that too. Anyway, can we bury the hatchet and start over?"

"You want to bury that hatchet between my shoulder blades or my eyes?" Michelle succeeded in keeping a straight face.

"Neither, for shit's sake. I'm sorry I took you for granted and then acted like an ass every time I came home at the end of hitch."

"I'm tired of fighting too, Georgie. We're all we have left that's family. I'm sorry I over reacted about Stacey. But, damn it, I'm the one at the ranch twenty-four-seven and you just waltz in and announce I'm supposed to be thrilled about living with a complete stranger. Not to mention one who has a history with my fiancé."

"I said I'm sorry, Michelle. What more do you want from me?" He stalked around the room.

"Sit down, you're making me dizzy." She patted the edge of the bed. "Look, the ranch is still half mine, but I'm happy living here with Cale, so if you and Stacey want to shack up over there it's fine with me."

George perched on the side of the bed. "So, you're not mad at me anymore? We're buds again?"

"Yeah, I guess." She grinned at him.

"Good. I hate it when you're pissed at me." He ruffled her hair, avoiding the bruise. "Now I can quit looking over my shoulder for whatever revenge you're planning."

"Until next time anyway." She blinked and rubbed her eyes.

"Look, I'm gonna go. You're tired and Cale'll have my head if I tire you out. Stacey says she hopes you feel better soon." George got up from the bed. "You take care okay? Call me if there's anything I can do to help."

"Thanks, bro. For an ass-wipe you can be a good big bro at times."

"Thanks, I think." He winked at her and disappeared into the hall.

Storm and Crazy Puppy set up a roar when he got to the kitchen. Michelle laid back and smiled. Cale's voice came clearly down the hall so the door must be open. "It's a bit late for that, mutts. He's already in. Settle down now." The conversation faded when the hall door snicked shut.

* * *

"You did what?" Cale glowered at her over the breakfast table. Three weeks had passed since the accident and Michelle was feeling back to normal. Although she'd rather have avoided this confrontation.

"I called Rolly and asked about outriding for him. He called earlier with the date for the testing."

"You've just up and decided you want to spend the summer outriding? It's dangerous, Michelle. You know that, and besides there's no female outriders that I know of."

"May Gorst did it, and she was good. One of the best." Michelle protested. "Milly Hamilton and Clarice Guard did too, back in

1951. What about Kaila Mussel? She rides rough stock. You think I'm not tough enough, or good enough?"

"Are you done?" Cale regarded her levelly. The only indication of his agitation was his fingers drumming on the table. "I have no doubt of your ability, or your craziness. I'm quite sure you could outride. My question is why would you want to?"

"Spud's treatment is expensive and Rain is too green to be able to win enough money…"

"Are you sure this is about the money? Doc and I both have told you not to worry about the bills. We'll take care of them and you can pay us back when you can if you insist on it. I think this is more about you proving to yourself you haven't lost your nerve. A head injury is a serious thing."

"I didn't hurt my head riding."

"I know that, Michelle. I'm just asking you to reconsider. I don't want to spend the summer without you. We haven't done any planning for the wedding yet, hell we haven't even set a date." He scrubbed a hand through his hair.

"You been talking to Mary? She's been on to me about setting a date too."

"No, this is coming from me. I love you and I don't want you running all over the place with the chucks."

"I already promised Rolly I'd do it. I just have to pass the test. I'm going out to his place tomorrow to practice with his team. I really want to do this." She set her chin in a stubborn line.

"I can't say I'm happy about it, but if you have your heart set on it there's not much I can do. I gotta get to the clinic. I'll see you tonight. Seriously, we need to sit down and figure out a date."

"Okay. I love you." Michelle stroked Storm's head and watched the truck's rooster tail of dust flare over the gravel road when Cale dipped into the coulee and came up the other side.

"He's right, Storm. I do want to get married, I just don't know when. What do you think? Maybe September? Maybe Christmas, or what about next spring?" The black dog tipped her head to the side and licked Michelle's hand. "You're no help." She ruffled the dog's fur and got up to clear the table.

If she was honest with herself, the thought of outriding sent butterflies galloping through her gut. Maybe Cale was right, maybe she call Rolly and say she couldn't do it. He'd understand. *Grampa always said a Wilson paid their own way in life. If you got into a fix, you got your own self out again. And never, never take money from friends.* The old man's words echoed in her head. "Tell you what Storm. I'm gonna take the outrider test and if I don't make it, well, that takes care of that doesn't it? If I get through it, then I'll do and do a few meets. If I really don't like it I'll just come home."

With that settled in her mind, Michelle tidied up the kitchen and went out to take care of the chores. She still had bouts of exhaustion, which she hid from Cale if she could, and only a tiny bit of a headache if she exerted herself too much. Doc Lewen said she was fine though and to get on with living her life. Which was just what she intended to do. The new cell phone in her hip pocket buzzed as crossed the yard to the barn. The old one never showed up, probably buried under a shitload of snow.

"Hello?"

"Are you out of your mind?" George's voice roared in her ear. She winced and held the phone away.

"What?"

"Have you lost your mind, Michelle?"

"I'm talkin' to you, so maybe."

"Don't be smart with me. You're not going outriding, you hear me? I won't let you."

"You won't let me?" Anger simmered and made her voice deceptively quiet.

"No, I won't." He sounded uncertain, as if he realized his mistake in the choice of words too late.

"You aren't the boss of me, big brother. I'll do whatever I want, and if outriding is one of them, then that's what I'm gonna do. Man, Cale didn't waste any time calling you did he?"

"Wasn't Cale, don't blame him for this one. Rolly called me this morning and mentioned it like I should already know about your harebrained idea."

Thanks Rolly. "I didn't think I needed to ask your permission. I wasn't going to say anything to anyone other than Cale until I knew if I passed the testing committee."

"There's that at least. Hopefully, they'll see reason and fail your ass."

"Thanks for the vote of confidence, George."

"I didn't mean it like that, Michelle. I just don't want to see you scraped up off the track and carted off in an ambulance."

"I'm smart, Rolly has good horses. Nothing bad is gonna happen."

"It's wagon racing, you know as well as me there's no guarantees."

"Can you at least think positive for me?"

"I'll never understand females. Stacey is higher than a kite, thinks you should go for it and show those boys how it's done. She's even talking about asking you to give her riding lessons and teaching her to barrel race. Damndest thing I ever heard."

"You tell Stacey I'd be happy to give her a lesson or two. Just get her to give me a call."

"You're really stuck on doing this, Michelle? I take it Cale isn't too keen on you risking your neck?"

"No, he's less than enthusiastic. I really want to do this, George. And I'm gonna give it my best shot. Just because I whacked me head, I can't spend the rest of my life worrying that I might hurt it again. I can't worry about what might happen."

177

"Well, if you're set on it, I won't give you any more grief. But, I sure don't have to like it."

The line went dead. Michelle held the phone out and stared at it for a moment before shaking her head and returning it to her pocket. Stacey was becoming more and more of an enigma. Who would have thought the blonde would be the one championing Michelle's cause to her brother and Cale. Would wonders never cease?

Chapter Twelve

"I did it! I can't believe I did it!" Michelle danced in circles with Stacey, laughing and almost crying at the same time.

"I knew you'd make it." Stacey crowed.

"Way to go, girl!" Rolly jumped down from the wagon as one of the crew caught the leaders as he pulled them to a halt. Grabbing her around the waist the little cowboy swung her around until her feet left the ground. "This summer is gonna be great. I can't wait to get goin' down the road."

"Put me down, you idiot." Michelle slapped him on the back until he set her back on the ground.

The other members of the team offered their congratulations as well before dispersing to take care of the horses. Rolly led the way toward a stack of hay just inside the barn door. He retrieved the thermos of coffee and poured three cups. "To a very successful summer!" He raised his cup in a toast and touched Michelle and Stacey's in turn.

"Why did Michelle have to do two runs? One throwing that thing into the wagon and the other holding the horses?" Stacey asked. "When I read the rules she should only have had to do one or the other. Was it because she's a girl and they wanted her to fail?"

Rolly shook his head. "I don't think that was why. Sometimes they make the guys do both. Especially if they don't already know them because they're part of a wagon family. The committee just didn't know Michelle that well, even if her dad used to race. They wanted to make sure she could handle either position. It's all about nobody getting hurt if we can help it."

"I suppose…" Stacey glanced at Michelle. She didn't look like she quite believed the explanation.

"Doesn't matter, I got the okay." Michelle grinned.

"When do you have to start? Did Cale know your test was today?" Stacey frowned.

"I told him. He didn't seem too excited about it though," Michelle replied.

"Is that gonna be a problem? You coming with me?" Rolly looked concerned.

She shook her head. "Nope. I'm looking forward to it. I can't run barrels with the girls, I might as well run them with the boys." She giggled.

"Not exactly the same thing. You know I support you in this, but what if you get hurt?" Stacey worried her bottom lip with her teeth.

"I'm not gonna get hurt," Michelle protested. "George and I used to race ponies in the chariot races when we were kids. I think I'd have more of a chance getting hurt in the wild pony race or mutton busting than the chucks."

"You're probably right." Rolly laughed. He stuck out his hand and shook Michelle's. "Welcome to the team. I gotta go help with the horses. I'll be in touch about GP once I get things set. See ya, Chelly. Nice to meet you, Stacey." The short cowboy hurried away.

"I can see why they call him Rolly." The blonde giggled, her eyes on his rolling gait. The man was definitely round and rolly polly.

"His name's actually Roland, but yeah, Rolly does suit him." Michelle smothered a grin.

"Oops, glad I didn't put my foot in it." Stacey put a hand over her mouth, blue eyes sparkling with mirth above it.

"Don't worry about it. He's heard it all about a thousand times over. It just rolls off his back like water off a duck."

"Aren't you going to call Cale and tell him the good news?"

"I'm not sure he's going to think it's good news. He'd rather I stuck around the ranch this summer and we haven't set a wedding date yet." Michelle scuffed the toe of her boot in the dust.

"Do you have a date in mind?" Stacey's expression brightened with excitement.

"Not really. I guess maybe I'm a bit gun shy after Rob and all. I'm really glad you came with me today. I was pretty nervous, having another girl here helped a lot."

"I'm glad you asked me to come. I really hope we can be friends. And, now that you and your brother are talking again maybe we can do a family dinner once a month?"

"Don't expect that to last too long, me and George not feuding I mean." Michelle laughed. "We've always been at each other's throats since we were kids. But a family dinner would be nice."

"Good. I'll start planning one. Maybe next Sunday before George goes back to the rig?"

"Sure, just let me know. C'mon, let's hit the road. If we get going we can stop at Pat's and you can have your first riding lesson on Rain."

"Really? That would be awesome. I hate that ATV, it'll be so much nicer checking the stock down in the coulee on horseback."

"Let's go then. We'll stop at Tim's on the way out town and get a coffee." Michelle slapped her hat on her thigh to knock the dust loose and strode toward the truck.

"Do you ever go anywhere without a Tim's?" Stacey followed on her heels.

"Nope." Michelle hopped in the cab and started the engine.

"It must be genetic, George is addicted to the stuff too." Stacey joined her in the truck.

* * *

"So you passed your outrider test?" Cale leaned back in his chair and watched her clear the dinner dishes.

182

"Yeah. It was great and Stacey was awesome." Michelle carried the dishes to the sink, stepping over Storm on the way.

"I'm glad you and Stacey are getting along. She's really a nice person if you'd just give her a chance."

"I'm finding that out. I gave her a lesson on Rain before we came home. She actually did pretty good."

"You're really set on this outrider thing? I'm worried about you, they don't call it the Half a Mile of Hell for nothing. What about stuff around here and planning our wedding? Hell, we haven't even agreed on a date yet." He set his coffee mug on the table.

"I promised Rolly I'd help out and yeah, I think it'll be fun. I haven't been around the rodeo for a while. I miss it."

"What about Rob, do you miss him too?" His voice was so quiet she had to listen closely to make out the words.

"Idiot! I don't miss that ass at all. The chucks run in the evenings, except at Strathmore this year. Rob will be long gone once the bulls are done." She crossed the room and threw her arms around his neck from behind. "I love you." She kissed his ear.

"So long as you don't forget that." Cale pulled her around to sit on his lap. "Now what about humoring me and setting a date for this wedding of ours?"

His lips captured hers and for a few minutes she forgot what they were talking about. "I don't know. Do we have to pick a date right now? I can think of other things I'd rather do."

"Wench, don't change the subject and try to distract me with your wiles." He tightened his arms around her.

"Okay, what about September?" She trailed kisses down his jaw.

"If you're gonna be gone all summer when are you planning to arrange things?"

"Hmmm, Mary would help. But maybe you're right, September isn't that far away. What about near Christmas? Maybe after the CFR?"

"Really, Christmas? Isn't that around the time you and that cowboy were supposed to get married?" Cale leaned back and studied her face.

"Yeah. I guess, I hadn't thought about that. Okay, when then? You suggest a good time." She frowned at him. Typical male to throw a monkey wrench into the works.

"I thought sometime in the spring might be nice. We can tell everyone at Christmas when we're all together. Mom and Dad are planning on coming to Mary and Doc's Christmas Eve do, and everyone else we need to tell will be there."

"Springtime? May would be nice, when the crocus are in bloom. I want some pictures with the coulee in the background and maybe down by the river. What do you think?" Tiny thrills of excitement twisted through her. Talking about marrying Cale and picking the date made it seem more real that it had before.

"Now we're getting somewhere. So, May of next year it is. Now we just need a date."

"How about the second week? I don't want to do it on the May long weekend. Too many people go away and there's always a rodeo to go to."

"May long might make it easier for anyone who has to travel though," Cale suggested.

"Anyone we really want to be there lives in town or nearby. There just seems to always be so much going on that weekend. The more I think about the more I like the second week of May."

"What's the date?"

"No clue. Where's the calendar?" Michelle disentangled herself from his lap and crossed the kitchen to get the calendar from by the phone. She flipped through the pages while she returned to the table. "Damn, this only goes to December."

"Look on the back, Chelly." Cale grinned, took the folder from her and flipped it over. "Next year is on the back." He handed it to her.

"Smart ass." She looked at the dates. "Second Saturday in May next year is the fourteenth, so I guess that's it." Michelle grinned at him over the top of the pages. "Happy?"

"Very." He swept her into his arms. "Very, very happy." Kisses punctuated each word.

"Me too." She said when they came up for air. "I'm gonna miss you this summer, but once I'm home I'm gonna start planning." She paused. "I'd like to keep it quiet for a while, if you don't mind? Once Mary gets wind of this she'll be like a dog with a bone. Before I know it, the wedding will be all planned out and I won't have had a say in it. You know how she gets."

"You're probably right about that. She does get the bit in her teeth. I don't mind not saying anything, as long as we're agreed that May fourteenth is the date. No changing our minds."

"Deal. You can tell Peggy and Carson if you think Mary won't get it out them."

"I'll think about it. I'm not sure Mom will be able to keep it quiet once she hears. She'll be pretty excited that we've decided on a definite date. Who are you going to have for a maid of honour? Mary? I guess she'd be a matron of honor?"

"I want Mary to be mother of the bride and Doc to give me away. I haven't asked either of them, but I don't think it will be an issue. What do you think?"

"I think they'd be upset if you didn't. Especially Doc. Mary will be happy either as matron of honour or honorary mother of the bride. So, who are you asking to be maid of honour? Pat?"

Michelle burst out laughing. "Are you kidding? Pat would kill me dead if I asked her to put on some frou frou dress. No, actually I was thinking of asking Stacey." She waited to see Cale's reaction.

"I think she'd like that," Cale said slowly. "Are you sure?"

"Yeah. I've been mulling it over, and we've been getting along pretty good."

"Since you gave her the benefit of the doubt?" Cale interrupted.

"Since she quit making calves' eyes at you, you mean," she countered.

"Whatever, have it your way."

"Anyway, her and George look like they're getting along. I mean, this is the longest my brother has ever stayed with any girl, let alone lived with one. She must be some kind of saint to put up with him."

"She really does seem to be in love with him," Cale agreed.

"How many guys are you asking? I guess I need to have the same number of girls as you have men."

"I hadn't really thought about it. I could ask George. I have a buddy from school, but if we keep it small and you're going to ask Stacey it makes sense for me to ask your brother. Are you okay with no bridesmaids?"

"The smaller the better as far as I'm concerned. I hate a big fuss and being the centre of attention. As long as you're there that's all that matters." She hugged him.

"A woman after my own heart." He kissed her nose. "Have you thought about where to get married?"

187

"The church in town? It's sorta traditional. It might be nice to have it outside here or over the coulee. But what if the weather doesn't cooperate?"

"It's only May, Chelly. It might snow for heaven's sake. I'd rather not be trying to say my vows with my teeth chattering."

"Good point. I'll check with Reverend Carter next time I'm in town and ask him to keep it under his hat."

"If we can't trust him who can we trust?" Cale grinned. "Now that's settled, tell me when you leave. It's Grande Prairie first, right?"

"Yeah, GP is the end of May, the last weekend. But I'll need to be over at Rolly's for a couple of weeks before that so I can practice and get to know the horses."

"He's just in High River though. You'll be home every night."

"Just try and keep me away." She grinned at him. "After that it's pretty steady. Saskatoon, The Hat, High River, and Ponoka, then Calgary. Can you believe I get to ride at the Stampede?"

"I just want you to be safe and have fun. If Carrie will cover for me, I'll be at High River and Ponoka. You'll have to keep in touch when you're on the road. You riding with Rolly?"

"Yeah. A lot of guys have their own RVs, but Rolly says it's no problem for me to ride shotgun with him. I'll get a hotel if there's one near the grounds or I can camp out in one of the portable stalls. Rolly's got dibs on the sleeper in the semi unless Sharon shows up with the RV."

188

"Just be careful, okay. I can't help worrying about you."

"It's not like I'm the only woman around. Most of the guys have their families with them, you know that."

"Indulge me, just promise me you'll be careful."

"Promise. You promise me you won't let your head get turned by some pretty little thing while I'm gone."

"You don't have to worry on that count. Even if I was tempted, which I won't be, Doc and Mary would nail my hide to the barn wall if I so much as looked at someone else."

"That's true." She laughed. "Mary would skin you alive and Doc would remove certain parts of your anatomy."

"Nice, Michelle. That sounds really reassuring." Cale mocked frowned at her.

"I do love you so much." She slid her arms around his waist. "Let's take the dogs out, check the stock for the night and go to bed."

"Sounds like a plan to me."

* * *

"Grande Prairie twenty kliks." Rolly read the highway sign out loud. "Getting' nervous, rookie?" He grinned across the cab at Michelle.

"Oh yeah. Nervous, scared, but in a good way," she assured him. "I hate the waiting part.

189

Once we get the horses hitched and the wagons start to roll I'll be fine."

"Lots of work to do before we get to the fun part," he reminded her.

"No kidding. I can't believe the amount of stuff you guys haul with you. Do we set up the portable stalls before we unload the horses or what?"

"We usually put up the temporary corrals first if there aren't any permanent ones and turn them out for a roll."

"Okay, just tell me what you need once we're there." She peered in the side mirror. "The boys are still right behind us with the other rig and the RVs."

"Reach in the back for the thermos, would you? I could use a coffee right about now." Rolly didn't take his eyes off the road.

Michelle undid her seatbelt and kneeled on the seat while she retrieved the large thermos. Unscrewing the top she poured most of what remained into Rolly's go mug. The rest she dumped in her own cup. "Thank God there's a Tim's in just about every town now."

"You got that right, girl." Rolly grinned and lifted his go mug in a solute before taking a healthy swig. "Ah, nectar of the gods."

Michelle sipped hers more sedately. The butterflies in her stomach were giving her fits. It wouldn't do for her to hurl all over the cab. *Damn nerves.* For a moment her thoughts drifted to dangers of wagon racing. Dick Cosgrave having that wreck at Kamloops back in '93, getting up out of the dirt and walking to the infield rail before he collapsed and died. George Normand at Ponoka. Bill McEwan. Her dad, but she'd rather not thing about that. Any number of wrecks came to mind. *But that's not going to happen. Think of all the races that go off with no problems.*

"What're you lookin' so serious about all of a sudden." Rolly glanced at her as he geared down to take the exit for Grande Prairie off 43 North. "We've hit all the high points so far. Whitecourt, Fox Creek, now there's a happenin' town, Valleyview. What more can a girl ask?"

"Oh be still my heart." Michelle placed her hand over her heart and grinned. "Nope, just nerves. I'll be fine once I get busy."

"No shame in admitting to a case of nerves. Happens to all of us. If I'm not half scared half-crazy with excitement before a race I don't have a good run."

"Thanks."

Silence filled the cab as Rolly navigated through the already busy streets. The city was filling up people coming from the outlying communities for the Grande Prairie Stompede. The rig turned into the Evergreen Park followed by the rest of their entourage. Michelle craned her neck trying to take it all in. The RVs turned off at the RV campground located on the grounds just past the public parking lots. Rolly continued on and followed the road as it swung around the far side of the track and then turned onto the lane toward the barns on the back side of the track. He pulled to a halt at the entrance to the stabling area to speak with the attendant in the guard shack. Michelle handed him the folder with the paperwork and the horse's health certificates which Rolly passed on to the guard.

"Everything's in order. Same barn as last year. Good luck and have a good meet, Rolly." The man slapped the truck door and lifted the cross arm to clear the lane.

"Thanks, Joe. See ya around." The truck eased into gear and moved forward.

It was all Michelle could do not to bounce up and down on the seat like ten year old kid. *I can't wait to call Cale and tell him how great this is.*

"Which barn are we in?" Michelle looked at the barns clustered by two outside dirt rings.

Rolly shoved the paperwork back at her. "We're over by the track, first barn in the back row as we come in."

She set the folder in the pocket on the door where it would be within easy reach. "I can't believe I'm really here."

Rolly laughed. "It's always fun watching a rookie get their first taste of it."

"Oh shut up." She slapped his arm playfully. "Park this damn thing and let's get this show on the road."

Hours later Michelle dropped into the cot she'd set up in the stall where they kept the feed and harness. All the horses were exercised, fed and watered, their stalls bedded with a thick layer of straw. The wagon parked nearby, all the tack and feed neatly stowed in the area around her. Her stomach wanted food and her body wanted to lie still for about a week.

"Hey, rookie. You coming into town to get some grub?" Hal, one of the guys who rode for Rolly stuck his head in the door.

"Yeah, just give me a second." She forced herself upright, the lure of food stronger than the need for sleep. In the end she was glad she'd gone with them. Some of the people she knew from barrel racing and following the rodeo with Rob. Others she didn't know were just as friendly. She took some good natured ribbing about her rookie status. She piled into the pickup with Hal and the other guys. They dropped her at the barns before heading back to the RV campground. Michelle had refused their offer to bunk in with them. It wasn't something she really wanted to explain to Cale, even though it was perfectly innocent. She waved them off and did one last check on the horses before falling into the cot fully clothed after pulling the stall door shut.

Dawn came early in May on the northern prairies. Michelle rolled out of bed around four-thirty when the eastern sky was turning gold and pink. The sun wouldn't be actually be up for about another hour, but there was enough light to see. The morning sounds of horses nickering for food and whinnying to each other mingled with the voices of the grooms and the clank of wheel barrows and pitchforks.

Rolly showed up just as Michelle finished filling the feed buckets in preparation of distributing them to the impatient horses. Without speaking Rolly began pitching hay into the stalls and she followed behind, putting the correct bucket in each horse's stall. While the horses ate Rolly produced a tray of coffee and a bag of breakfast sandwiches.

"Gotta feed the help," he quipped.

"Thanks, man. I'd kill for a coffee right about now."

They ate in silence. Michelle leaned her head against the side of the barn, her feet stuck out in front of the bale of hay she was sitting on. Crumpling up her food wrapper she collected Rolly's and dumped the garbage in the trash bin.

"Sit down and finish your coffee." Rolly seemed reluctant to move from his perch on a hay bale on the opposite side of the feed stall door.

Happy to steal another few minutes of peace and quiet before mucking out the stalls, she settled back on the recently vacated bale and nursed the last dregs of liquid from the cardboard cup.

The sun was well up and the rest of the crew began showing up, wandering in from the RV campground looking a little bit the worse for wear from the night before.

"Time to get cracking." Rolly got to his feet and stretched.

Michelle tossed her cup out and hurried to help brush the horses. Rolly came down the shed row with a list of which horses he wanted hitched for the first night and which outrider horses were going to go that evening. The others would get a light workout later in the day.

She'd harnessed before but it took her a few minutes to make sense out of the traces and the lines. One mistake could result in a horrendous wreck and she was acutely aware of the need to get everything correctly placed. Rolly rechecked everything once the team was hooked. Michelle went to get the rangy chestnut gelding she was to ride. The light saddle sat nose down outside the stall with the pad lying on top. With quick sure movements she settled them on his back and tightened the cinch. She snatched the bridle from the hook outside the stall and slipped it on his head. The horse followed her eagerly out of the stall. He knew his job and the crisp morning air made him want to run. He curveted around her while Michelle took the helmet Hal tossed her and fastened in under her chin.

Rolly swung up into the driver's seat and took the team toward the track. The barrels were set in the figure eight pattern in the infield in front of the grandstand. A few other wagons were already circling the track. Michelle vaulted onto the gelding and laughed as he danced beneath her. "Soon enough, Hank. Soon enough."

Rolly waved her up beside the wagon and she let the horse lengthen his stride until she came even with the driver's seat. "Hal's gonna take the leaders. You take the stove."

She nodded and dropped back. When the way was clear Rolly took the team through the figure eight at a controlled pace. Michelle noted he took care to keep the leaders from ducking in toward the first barrel. He'd drawn the number one barrel and wanted to make sure the horses didn't get distracted turning past the chutes. He pulled the horse to a jigging walk and Hal nodded to the other two riders. Rolly halted the horses with the front wagon wheel beside the barrel. Hal jumped down and took hold of the leaders. The rear wagon wheel couldn't be in front of the barrel when the horn blew or there'd be at least a one second penalty. Michelle vaulted off and lined up behind the wagon, holding Hank with one hand and the other on the barrel. Rolly gave the signal and Michelle heaved the light barrel that served as substitute for the stove. It landed in the back of the wagon with a satisfying thump. Hal had already released the lead team and gotten onboard his horse. Michelle vaulted onto Hank and keeping an eye out for the other riders and the wagon wove through the figure eight pattern and followed the wagon out of the infield.

Rolly pulled them up half way down the back stretch. The two riders trotted alongside.

"You did good, Michelle. You okay or do you want to do it again?"

"I think I've got it. Unless you guys think I should do it one more time?" She waited for the two men to pass judgement on her performance.

196

Hal shrugged and looked to Rolly's brother Clay. "I didn't see what went on behind, but she stayed out of the way."

"Looked good to me," Clay said from his perch on the chutes.

"Okay then. I'm gonna take these guys easy around the rail. I'll meet you back at the barn and we can get these guys put away and give the other horses their workout."

Michelle let Hank canter back to the barn, her feet swinging free of the stirrups. Adrenaline thrummed through her body. It was euphoric. She whooped and grinned at her companions.

"Oh, oh. Looks like the rookie's hooked," Clay joked. She liked Rolly's brother even if he was a bit of a clown sometimes.

"Another adrenaline junky." Hal shook his head.

"Like you should talk," she shot back.

"You couldn't pay me to tear around out there," Clay declared. "I like my skin in one piece."

Back at the barns she stripped the chestnut and rubbed him down, taking care to make sure there was no heat or swelling in the legs. It took the better part of the morning to get through all the horses. Then the tack and harness all had to be checked for loose stitching or anything else that might need repairs. Michelle busied herself cleaning tack after throwing the horses their noon hay and checking water. All the animals seemed to be in good form. The backstretch settled into afternoon quietness. A few kids played in front of the barns and country music played in one of the shed rows. Rolly had gone back to his RV for a nap. Hal and Clay had disappeared as well. She guessed they had gone off either to nap or go into town.

Laying down the bridle she was soaping, Michelle fished out the bag with her lunch form behind the bale. Greasy burger and fries from the midway concessions. She grinned, nothing better. Wolfing it down, she finished with the tack. If she were smart she'd try and get some rest before things picked up again in preparation for the evening races. Michelle was too keyed up to rest so she occupied herself with brushing a couple of the younger horses and then wandered down the shed row to gossip with one of the driver's wives that she knew.

Rolly showed up around two-thirty. The first heat was scheduled for five in the afternoon. Before long the activity in the backstretch increased as more and more outfits started to gear up for the evening's performance. Michelle helped Rolly go over the wagon one more time, checking the wheel hubs and the wagon tongue connection to the bed of the chuck.

"We're not til the fifth heat so we've got a bit of time." The short-legged cowboy leaned against the side of the wagon and stretched out his back. "Man, I swear I feel like a hundred years old sometimes."

"All that clean livin' you do," Michelle teased him. "Try hittin' the sack before three am."

"No sense livin' if you're not really livin'." He grinned at her, removed his hat and scrubbed his face before replacing it.

"You got that flak jacket your boyfriend made me promise to make you wear?"

"Awe, c'mon Rolly. You aren't really gonna make me wear that thing are you?" Michelle grimaced. It was bad enough being a rookie without wearing a flak jacket like some kid in the mutton busting.

"Bull riders wear 'em, as well you know." He gave her the evil eye.

"Yeah, yeah. But I'm not ridin' a bull." She gave up protesting when he shook his head.

"No jacket, no outriding. A promise is a promise."

"Fine." She huffed her disapproval.

Suddenly the time flew by. The wagons for the first heat rattled out onto the track, followed by the klaxon horn and the roar of the crowd. The four wagons rolled down the backstretch throwing up clods of dirt. They rounded the far turn three wide across the track.

"The louder you cheer, the sooner they get here," Les McIntyre exhorted the crowd.

Michelle blocked out the extraneous noise while she concentrated on helping to hook the wheel team and then the leaders. The big bay right wheeler snorted and tossed his head. She knew he liked to jump ahead and get the wagon by the barrel before the leaders turned. Hank was already saddled and waiting in his stall. She ran to get him and followed Hal out onto the groomed track.

Her heart pounded so hard it was difficult to breathe. She registered the brightly coloured crowd as a single blur as they entered the infield. It was a lot more crowded with the other three wagons and their outriders taking their practice turns on the barrels. The announcer introduced each wagon and the canvas sponsor. Michelle couldn't remember who Rolly's sponsor was. *It doesn't matter. Concentrate.* Her knees almost gave way when she vaulted off Hank and took her place at the back of the wagon.

"Ready to cast your fate to the figure eight?" Rolly glanced back to be sure she was in place. His breath came fast and his eyes gleamed with excitement.

She didn't have a chance to respond as the horn blared and together they threw the stove into the bed of the wagon. The roar of the crowd was drowned out by the rattle of four wagons and the pounding of sixteen horses as they negotiated the tight turns around the barrels. Michelle made a pony express mount onto the rangy chestnut and managed to get him around the barrels before they were out and into the first turn. The thin white jacket that identified her as the wagon on the number one barrel's outrider snapped in the wind. She leaned low over the horse's neck and whooped for the sheer joy of riding at break neck speed alongside the wagons. Careful to stay clear of the wagons she kept an eye on where Rolly was placed in the crush of horses as they rounded the turn and lengthened out down the back stretch. The drivers jockeyed for position, some trying to find room to snug in to the rail Rolly had his team running just off the rail and in front of the pack. To her left, Hal was letting his horse run and sitting still for the moment. They needed to stay close to their wagon, crossing the finish line without being within 150 feet of the wagon was a one second penalty. It might not seem like much but when races were often by tenth of a second and the aggregate at the end of a meet could result in a big pay day, one second could be the difference between first and tenth place.

The voices of the drivers rose in a crescendo as they rounded the third turn and ran for home. They slapped the lines on the horses' back to encourage them. It was more excitement on the driver's part as the horses were only too happy to run at top speed. She moved Hank out away from a wagon that was going wide in an attempt to catch Rolly at the wire. The horse responded when she leaned lower and touched him with the crop she pulled out of her boot. He didn't need any more encouragement, the horse lowered himself and stretched out into a longer stride. The announcer's voice was lost in the screams of the crowd and thunder of the hooves. Michelle swept under the wire and stood in her stirrups, convincing Hank the race was over and he needed to slow down. He broke into a trot as Rolly slowed the wagon team and turned them back to parade in front of the grandstand. Clay's friends leaped into the back of the wagon and took the lines from him. The group of outriders followed the four wagons back into the outfield and then saluted the crowd as they left.

Back at the barns, Michelle didn't have any time to reflect on her first race. The steaming wagon horses needed to be unharnessed and washed down, then walked until they cooled off. Likewise for the outrider horses. Some of the men were outriding for more than one outfit. She peeled off the white jacket and handed it to the track official who would pass it to the next rider. Hal and Clay disappeared to collect their mounts for the following heat and Michelle took care of their horses as well as her own.

She finished in time to watch the last heat of the night. She whooped with the rest as Jason's and Troy's team swept past the finish line neck and neck. Later that night she joined the party, sitting on hay bales in front of the stalls, laughing and talking with the close knit community. It felt good to be part of the comradery again. She hadn't realized how much she missed this. When she was little she used to sit on Dad's knee until she fell asleep, long before the festivities wound down. He'd be proud of her, following the family tradition of wagon racing. The fact he'd died after being thrown from his wagon when the team beside his went down had taken her away from the sport. Gramma and Grampa didn't want to be around it and Michelle had only been eight at the time. Over the years she'd forgotten the closeness of the chuck wagon community.

The rest of the meet flew by, the thrill of racing with the wagons increased with each ride. She could well understand how addicting the experience was. Just about anything else paled in comparison. Cale might not be too thrilled, but Michelle thrived on walking that thin line between triumph and disaster. She called him every night after the races to let him know how they were doing and how much she missed him.

Michelle tacked up a rangy grey gelding in preparation for the last night of the meet. They were racing in the championship heat. Her hands fumbled with the cinch strap. There was a lot of money riding on this race. She'd already made four hundred from the last four nights and Rolly promised bonus money if they won it all. Spud was healing, but Cale wanted him to have more shock wave treatments. He was worried the gelding might need surgery to repair the ligament damage. More money she didn't have at the moment. It was fine for Doc and Cale to say not to worry, Michelle was brought up to pay her own way. She hated taking money from anyone, even Doc and Cale.

"Chelly, let's go," Hal called as Rolly's wagon rattled down the shed row on the way to the track.

"Coming," she answered and brought the big horse out, vaulting into the saddle as soon as he was clear of the door. The gelding snorted and reared. She put her heels into him and sent him forward. "Settle down you jackass," she hissed at him. "Save it for the track."

She had her hands full with him in the infield. He pushed into her with his chest, swiveling his head, eyes wide and nostrils flared, as he stared at the crowd. He jerked her arm and stepped on her foot at the same time the horn went. "Bastard," she cursed. Thankfully, she managed to keep hold of the stove and it landed in the wagon bed. The grey reared again and she wasted precious time to haul him down, no sooner were his front feet on the dirt than she threw herself onto this back. Barely in control she managed the figure eight, her knee brushed a barrel but it stayed upright. Then they were tearing down the track chasing the wagons and outriders who had beaten her out of the infield. Michelle gave him his head and rode low over his neck to make up time. Near the end of the back stretch she pulled even with Hal. Rolly was three wide across the track ahead of them taking the long way around the track. *I hope they have enough gas left for the home stretch.* They pounded around the last turn and headed for home. Jordie's team on the rail seemed to be pulling ahead a bit. It was hard to tell with the dirt thrown up the hooves in front of her. She pulled the grey a bit wider and let him out a notch. She couldn't pass her wagon, but she sure wasn't gonna be a late outrider. She glanced over her shoulder Hal was a half a length behind her. *Looking good!* They swept past the finish and she concentrated on getting the grey lunkhead slowed down.

"Did we win?" She barely had the breath to talk.

Hal shrugged as he cantered beside her. She cuffed the grey gelding on the neck as he snapped his teeth at Hal's mount.

"Where'd he find this thing? He's fast as greased lightning, but what a pig."

"Don't know. I think he traded something for him. We'll see how he works out." Hal eased his horse to a trot.

They joined the parade past the grandstand. Rolly finished second by a nose. Still good money, but the bonus would have been better if they'd won.

She related it all to Cale later that night after the horses were cared for. They were packing up in the morning and heading for Saskatoon. No time for a quick visit home. Cale was understanding but she knew he wasn't thrilled.

June was full of travel. After a less than stellar performance at Saskatoon they headed south to Medicine Hat, finally, in the middle of May, they pulled into the familiar High River Rodeo Grounds. Cale was waiting for her when the truck stopped behind the stands. Michelle jumped out of the cab into his arms.

"I have missed you so much." She kissed him hard.

"I miss you too. It's good to see you. Hey, Rolly." Cale disengaged himself from her arms but kept a hold of her hand.

"Hey Cale. Thanks for lending me your lady here. She's making a name for herself as an outrider. I'm mighty proud of her."

"So am I." He smiled down at her and her stomach flipped. Michelle couldn't wait to get him alone. "Carrie's on call so I'm all yours. What needs doing?"

"C'mon, you can help me set up the rope corrals and get the horses off the trailer." Michelle pulled Cale along by the hand. "Rolly and the boys will set up the portable stalls under the roll out canopy. They'll be done by the time we're finished. Then they need to be fed and watered. But after that, I'm all yours," she promised.

He tugged her to a halt and kissed her til her toes curled in her boots. "I'm holding you to that." Cale grinned and pulled her pony tail. "Just show me what needs to be done."

The extra pair of hands and the promise of spending time alone with Cale hurried the chores along. Michelle waved to the boys gathered shooting the breeze with a good supply of wobbly pops to keep them going. She grinned at the mildly ribald comments thrown her way.

"See you in the morning!"

"I miss you, Chelly." Cale squeezed her hand.

"I miss you like crazy too. And the dogs and the horses and just being at the ranch. But,

Cale, running with the chucks is better than I ever imagined it! It's like...I don't know how to describe it...it's scary, but that's what makes it so much fun. If that makes any sense."

"Just don't get too addicted to it. I don't want to be chasing my wife all over hell's half acre once we're married." He took his attention from the road for a moment to look at her.

"It's not something I want to do forever." She paused as an idea popped into her mind. "Unless I could be a driver. That would be so cool." Michelle swivelled her body in the seat to face the driver. "Wow, wouldn't that be something?"

"Think about the cost. Those wagons aren't cheap, not to mention the horses and the gear."

She sighed and subsided back into the seat. "I know, and the rigs to go down the road with. It was a nice pipe dream while it lasted."

"How about you just enjoy it for now. The dogs will be glad to see you. Storm mopes around the house looking for you all the time." Cale changed the subject.

"I can't wait to see them. It's nice to be home, even if it's only for a couple of nights."

She leaned forward as the truck came out of the dip in the road and the ranch came into sight. It was one of those gold and blue Alberta evenings when the slanting rays of the sun lit the prairie with a golden orange hue burning against the clear blue of the big sky. She glanced at Cale before returning her gaze to the land. "I don't know why anyone would want to live anywhere else."

"Except when it's fifty below and the wind is blowing snow everywhere." Cale grinned.

"Be serious. Even then it's beautiful." She laid a hand on his arm. "How's Stacey doing? George must be back at work by now."

"She doesn't complain but I think she's finding it a bit lonely. The Gleason boy comes by to help with the heavy stuff. Stacey's learning to drive the big tractor but I think it scares the living daylights out of her," Cale replied.

"At least she's got some help. More than George ever did for me. Course I wasn't sleeping with him either. Ewwww." Michelle giggled. "Now there's a mental picture that'll put you off sex for a while."

Cale parked by the house and pulled her into his arms. "It better not. I have plans for you, woman. Wicked plans." His lips were warm and demanding on hers.

"Mental slate wiped clean," she managed to say when they came up for air. "Do we need to do chores?"

"Nope, all taken care of. Rain is in the lower pasture, Spud's still at the clinic though. I guess we should have stopped so you could see him tonight."

"Not a chance. Once Mary got a hold of me we'd be there all night and the only person I want to see right now is you." She kissed him again and got out of the truck. "C'mon, time's a'wasting!" Michelle ran for the door.

Cale was right behind her and caught her around the waist. He swung her up into his arms and kicked the outer door open. "Not exactly our wedding night, but…" She silenced him with her lips, winding her arms around his neck.

He shoved open the inner door and set her down when the dogs swarmed around his legs. "Down, Puppy. Easy, Storm," Cale attempted to calm the excited canines.

Michelle dropped to her knees and gathered them into her arms. The dogs wriggled and jockeyed for a better position eventually toppling her over onto her back with the two animals laying across her, licking wildly. "Okay, okay. I'm happy to see you too. Stop…Oh, yuck, stop that!" She got a hand free to wipe her face after Crazy Puppy slobbered on her, his tongue swiping across her mouth and nose. Taking the proffered hand she let Cale pull her to her feet. He used his thumb to remove some of the dog spit from her cheeks.

"Well, I've been fantasizing about licking you all over, I just wasn't picturing the mutts doing the licking." He grinned and pulled her close.

Heat flooded her body and she fitted her hips closer to his, smiling as she encountered his hardness. "I've got a few fantasies of my own to live out tonight. It's been too long time since I saw you naked as a jail bird." She wriggled against him and giggled. Cale picked her up and slung her over his shoulder. Michelle squealed in mock protest and tormented him by running her hands over his butt. He careened off a wall in the hall.

"Quit it, Chelly. We'll both be on the floor if you keep it up," he warned.

She worked her hand down the back of his jeans and under his boxers, squeezing his bare butt cheek.

"Jesus, Michelle." The words hissed between his teeth. "Two can play that game." One hand grabbed her ass and then followed the back seam of her jeans into the heat between her thighs.

Cale bounced off the doorframe of the bedroom while her head swam with the delicious sensations his fingers were drawing from her flesh. He let her slide down the front of his body, both hands firmly on her butt. Turning, he fell back on the bed pulling her with him.

"Welcome home, Chelly."

Chapter Thirteen

The High River meet was over way too soon for Michelle. The racing was exciting and way more than she had ever anticipated, but she missed being home with Cale. She lingered by the rig, savouring a last few minutes with him while the rest of the team loaded the last of the gear.

"I wish you weren't going." He removed her ball cap and brushed the loose strands of hair behind her ear.

"I know, me too. It's only Ponoka, though. Maybe you can come up and spend a night or two?"

"Maybe. Carrie covered for me this weekend though and next week is the July long weekend. She probably has plans."

"I know, I'm just being selfish. I won't be able to get away long enough to come home. Try and come up and watch at least one night?"

"I'll try. No promises. Doc might cover for me, but I don't want to ask him. Mary's just about got the old goat to only come out to the clinic a couple of days a week. And then mostly to consult."

"Good for Mary. She's the only one on this earth who has a shot of making that man see sense." She sobered. "I can't even think about losing him."

"Then don't. Think about Ponoka and Calgary."

She brightened. "I know! Calgary, can you believe it? I'm gonna ride at the big show. I always thought it'd be in barrels, but..." She shrugged and grinned.

"Personally, I'd rather it was barrels. Ride safe." He kissed her.

Rolly slammed the rig door on his side and tapped the horn. "Quit makin' out and get your ass in the truck." He threw her door open and grinned down at her.

"Comin' boss." She gave Cale one last kiss and hopped up into the cab. "I'll call you tonight. Love you."

Cale waved and his lips moved, but the words were lost in the engine's roar.

The dust rose in clouds as they pulled out of the grounds. "Man, it's been a dry spring," Michelle remarked.

"Yeah, hay's gonna be expensive if we don't get some moisture soon," Rolly agreed.

"I guess anything under irrigation has a chance, but that costs too. Our hayfield isn't doing much right now."

They lapsed into silence. Michelle watched the fields flash by as they drove north on 2A, hooking onto Highway 2 at Aldersyde and then catching Stoney Trail rather than driving through the heart of Calgary. Just south of Balzac, Rolly rejoined the main highway.

"Christ, that's a huge mall," he remarked as they passed Cross Iron Mills.

"Yeah, remember when that was all pasture? Not that long ago." Michelle frowned.

"Progress, woman. You can't halt progress," Rolly quipped.

They halted in Airdrie to pick up a fast food lunch. "This is the weirdest set up." Michelle waved at the city that was in effect divided in two by the busy highway.

"Whoever planned the place should be fired," Rolly agreed.

"Can't imagine living here. It must be hell at rush hour, there's only two overpasses and the place keeps growing." She shook her head.

Rolly wolfed down the last bit of burger and Michelle gathered up the wrappers and jumped down to throw them in the trash. The truck was rolling almost before she had her seatbelt fastened. "On to Ponoka!"

"You know, I heard somewhere that Ponoka means Elk in Blackfoot. They used to travel that far to hunt elk," Michelle broke the silence as they passed the Olds exit.

"Well aren't you little Miss Trivia," Rolly teased.

"I don't even know why I remembered that."

As they approached Alberta Downs just outside Lacombe the sun disappeared behind clouds gathering ahead of them. "Looks like we might get a storm," Rolly observed.

"Could use the moisture, I guess," Michelle answered. A tendril of fear wound through her. So far the tracks had been fast and dry. Running

213

in mud was a different thing altogether. "As long as it doesn't bucket down."

"I've got a team that likes to run in the mud. If we get weather in Ponoka I'll hook them. Don't worry, Chelly. A little mud never hurt anyone." He patted her knee.

Just after they took the 2A exit approaching Morningside, the skies opened. Torrents of rain lashed the windshield and the wind shook the big truck. "Shouldn't last long, not when it rains like this," Rolly assured her.

Thunder rolled across the sky right on the heels of the forks of lightning. They were right under the storm. Michelle checked the side mirror, the huge tires threw up a spray off the pavement. Combined with the rain sluicing down, she couldn't see if the other rig was still behind them or if Hal had pulled off.

It was still pouring when they drove into the stampede grounds. It was wet cold work setting up the stalls and getting the horses settled. Thank God she had a hotel room. She walked over to the infield with Rolly and a bunch of other people. The two huge grandstands sandwiched the groomed expanse of ground. Water was already pooling at the foot of the stands. Michelle hunched her shoulders under the oilskin jacket she wore. Water ran off it in streams, her feet inside her boots were damp and cold. She walked out into the centre of the infield with the rest and tested the footing. Although the top layer was slop underneath the footing was solid.

The stampede maintenance guys would work hard to keep the track safe. Michelle didn't envy them the long hours of grooming it would take to accomplish that. It would suck if she didn't get to ride. Her sense of adventure reared its head and the thought of racing in the flying mud was exciting. *Man, maybe I have some deep seated death wish or something. Some shrink would have a hay day with me.* She grinned wryly.

"What do you think? They'll get it in shape for the rodeo tomorrow afternoon?" Michelle asked Rolly.

He tipped his head back sending a stream of water cascading off the rim at the back of his hat. "If the damn rain lets up. If it keeps up like this…I don't know."

The group left the soggy area, some of the kids splashing and sliding in the slop squealing with delight. Some of the bigger ones got into a mudslinging fight, and caught up in the hilarity, Michelle joined in. Soon everyone, young and old alike, was covered in mud and laughing like hyenas.

"Shit, I haven't had that much fun with my boots on in a long time," one of the Bens boys remarked wiping mud out of his eyes.

Giving the horses one last check, topping water buckets and filling hay nets was a cold thankless task in the wind driven rain. Michelle was happy to pile into a pickup with a bunch of other wagon people and head to Dalton's for some grub. She was even happier that she

215

hadn't canceled the hotel room she'd booked when she expected to racing Spud at Ponoka. Her phone buzzed and she pulled it out of her pocket. It was Allie, asking if she could bunk with Michelle the next night. She texted back with the hotel and said she'd give the room number once she checked in.

At the lounge it looked like everyone was settling in for the night. Laughter and high spirits echoed in the room. Full of dinner and finding her eyes starting to droop, Michelle said her good nights. She stepped out of the restaurant and pulled the collar of her oilskin up around her neck while snugging her hat down further over her ears. It was only a short walk to the hotel but she was wet and shivery by the time she entered the lobby. The woman behind the front desk must have been used to clientele that were covered in dirt and smelled like horses. She didn't blink an eye while she took care of the paperwork and handed Michelle her room key. Clutching her drenched duffle bag Michelle found her room and thankfully stripped off her wed clothes. A hot shower helped improve her mood a great deal.

Snug and warm under the duvet with a paper cup of hotel room coffee on the bedside table she called Cale. The phone rang so long she almost gave up when he answered.

"'Lo?"

"Cale? Where are you? I can hardly hear you."

"Michelle? Is that you? The reception is shitty." There was a rustling and static crackling in her ear. "There, is that better?" His voice came though clearer.

"Yeah. Where are you? What's going on?" Concern made her sit up straighter against the pillows piled behind her.

"Out on a call. It's storming really bad."

"It's raining here too. We drove through a pretty big thunderstorm on the way up here."

"I'm just about at the call, Chelly. Where are you staying?"

"I'm at the hotel. Don't worry. Do you want me to call you later or do you want to call after you're done with the call?"

The rain drumming on the hood of the truck almost drowned out his words.

"I'll try to call later. I can't hardly hear you for the damn rain. You be careful, don't do anything stupid, you hear me?"

"Love you. Talk to you later." Michelle broke the connection. It must be raining worse down south than it was in Ponoka. Although the rain was still hitting the window with enough strength for her to hear it through the closed drapes, the wind seemed to have dropped and no thunder rolled through the downpour. She turned on the TV and watched a mindless sitcom while she finished her coffee. It was awful stuff, but it was hot at least. She set the empty cup on the bedside table and snuggled further down in the warmth of the bed. Her wet clothes were hung on the back of the desk chair in the room. Michelle had taken the hair dryer to them earlier and they were mostly dry. She tried Cale a couple more times but his phone went straight to voice mail. Either he was still out on calls or it was storming worse than she realized.

When she opened her eyes again the red numerals on the clock radio told her it was six am. *Cale never called back last night. Unless I didn't hear the phone?* The phone was hidden in the folds of the blankets, but when she finally unearthed it there were no missed calls showing and no texts. *Damn, I hope nothing's wrong and he was just really late.* By the time she showered and dressed it was just after seven. Cale's cell went straight to voice mail again and there was no answer on the land line at the ranch. Worry and frustration warred with each other. In desperation Michelle tried Mary. Surely she would be home at this time of the morning.

"Mary, it's me." A surge of relief washed over her. "What's going on? I can't reach Cale."

"Michelle, you still in Ponoka?"

"Yeah, where's Cale?" Worry sharpened her tone.

"The boy's fine. Carrie and him were out all night at a wreck. A cattle liner went off the road in storm. It was a mess. He's right here, asleep in the spare room."

"Thank God he's okay. Those poor cows though. Did any of them make it?" She sat on the side of the bed.

"A few. You know what Carrie did?"

"I can only guess."

"After they got the live ones out of the wreck and caught the loose ones she up and refused to let them put them on another truck and take them to the abattoir."

"Really?" Michelle laughed. "I can imagine how that went over with the drivers."

"The girl stood her ground, I have to give her that. Called one of the Hanson boys she's got friendly with and asked him to come with his stock trailer."

"So what happened?" Michelle shook her head.

"She got the owner on the phone and bought the ten head of cattle from him. Told him she'd give him slaughter price for them and not a penny more."

"So where are these cattle with nine lives now?"

Mary burst out laughing. When she got control of herself she managed to get the words out between giggles. "Your place. Cale let her put them in the corrals near the barn. That girl's soft heart is gonna get her in trouble if she doesn't toughen up."

"Oh great. Just what I need, ten pet cows. They are cows, right? No bulls?"

"Don't know. I think there's a couple of heifers, along with a few old girls who were being culled 'cause they came up open. Maybe a steer or two." Mary was still chuckling. "Doc said she was a sight. Hair all straggling in her face, blood everywhere and rain running off her like a duck. He said he sure wasn't about to cross her at that point."

"Well, good for her, I guess. Is she planning on keeping the things out at the ranch?"

"Don't know. Cale was just about falling down when he got here. Carrie brought your dogs in to the clinic after her and the Hanson boy dropped the cattle at your place."

"How bad is it there? How high's the river?" She thought about the stock down in the coulee.

"It's all right for now. Let's hope this weather doesn't stick around for too long."

"No kidding. Let Cale know I called when he wakes up. I don't know if they'll run tonight or not. No sense him driving up here in this crap."

"I'll let him know. You be careful, you hear."

"Yes, Mary." She grinned as she broke the connection.

* * *

The wagons rolled in the slop that night. Rolly's mudders came through for him and they finished first in their heat and won day money with the best over all time. Everyone pitched in to wash the horses and take down the mud tails. Michelle brushed the tangles out of the last one and pitched the wet brush into the pail by the

220

stall door. Clay and a few other guys who helped Rolly were busy cleaning harness, checking stitching and looking for worn or stretched leather that needed repair. She did a last check on the horses before collapsing on a bale of straw near the others in the shelter of the canopy on the side of the horse van. Dick handed her a mug of coffee and she wrapped her cold hands around it before lifting it to her mouth.

"Thanks, man, I'm half frozen."

"Not a fit night out for man or beast, as my grampa used to say." Clay grinned and continued cleaning the harness in his lap.

"Do we have some more goggles for tomorrow? I think I lost about four pair out there tonight," Michelle asked.

"Should be lots in the trunk," Hal replied. "I couldn't even see by the time we got to the wire."

"Have you heard the weather report? How long is the rain supposed to last?" Rolly joined them and set down a couple of big bags of burgers and fries. "Supper."

"The guy on the radio said it should ease up by noon tomorrow," Dick spoke around a mouthful of food.

"Let's hope they're right for a change." Rolly tossed his burger wrapper into an empty bag.

Once their hunger was taken care of no one wanted to hang around the rain soaked barn area. Michelle caught a ride back to the hotel and found Allie waiting for her when she got to her room. In typical Allie fashion, clothes and other paraphernalia was strewn on every available surface. She stepped over a pair of boots and closed the door.

"I see you've made yourself to home," she greeted her friend.

"Hey, you look like something the cat dragged in. I hope the infield isn't as muddy tomorrow. Shit, I hate running in the muck."

"I'm gonna shower and change." Michelle threaded her way through the mess to the bathroom. She picked up a pair of Allie's jeans off the toilet seat and tossed them out onto the floor of the room. Wasting no time she stripped off her dripping clothes and stood under the shower, letting the hot sting of the shower ease the knots in her muscles and warm her up.

With a towel wound around her head and another around her body Michelle joined her friend. Pulling on sweats and a heavy shirt she settled cross legged on the bed Allie hadn't claimed as her own. "So, fill me in. I haven't had a chance to really follow how the ladies are running."

"We're doing okay. Not as good as I'd like, but we've turned in some respectable times and won a little cash. Tell me about you. What's it like running with the crazies? I can't imagine charging around out there on a wild thoroughbred."

"I must be crazy, 'cause I love it. There's no feeling quite like it. I can't even explain it, it's so awesome."

"What does lover boy think of you chasing all over the place?"

"He's okay with it." She shrugged. "He's not thrilled, but he's okay with it."

The two girls spent a few hours exchanging gossip and catching up with each other before turning in.

* * *

The weather cleared for the rest of the meet. Michelle couldn't believe how quickly it was over. Once the sun came out she forgot about the unpleasantness of being wet and cold and covered in mud. Before she knew it they were taking down the portable stalls and packing up the gear. It was the first of July and the sky was alight with fireworks. She stopped and watched the display for a few minutes. They were headed to Calgary and the Stampede next. She had to pinch herself to be sure it was real. Vague childhood memories came to mind. She didn't remember much clearly from when Dad raced. Blurs of colour, a lot of noise and of course the horses. She remembered them the best. Michelle used to love to climb up on the chutes with the other kids and watch the barrel racers. They looked so amazing, like princesses she'd thought as a child.

A final burst of fireworks illuminated the area and she turned back to the job at hand. Calgary! Carrying the last tote she stowed it in the storage compartment and pulled out her cell phone to call Cale.

"Hey sweetie. I'll be in Calgary tomorrow. Any chance of you coming up?"

"Hey Michelle." He sounded preoccupied.

"What's wrong? Is Spud okay? Is it Doc?" The words spilled out in a rush.

"What? No, they're both fine. It's just been raining here again and the river's up. If it keeps rising I'll have to bring the stock up from the lower pastures."

"Is it that bad? It stopped here Saturday morning."

"Not yet, but if it keeps coming down…"

"Do you need me to come home?" She hated the thought of giving up racing in Calgary but the ranch had to come first.

"I don't think so. I've got things under control for now and the neighbors are all watching out for each other so even if I'm not here all the time we should be okay. You go ride and get it out of your system."

"Are you going to be able to come up at all?" Michelle tried to keep the disappointment out of her voice.

"I'm on call this weekend, but I should be there on Monday."

"I'm so glad. I can't wait to see you, I miss you like crazy."

"Me too. The dogs miss you too. Spud's getting stronger all the time. I've got one of Harvey's granddaughters hand walking him. I thing she can start riding him at a walk in the next day or so. She's a little thing, hardly weighs anything."

"That's a relief. Thank you so much for taking care of him for me. I've got a fair bit of money saved in case he still needs the surgery. If we do well at Calgary it'll really help the cause. And if Spud doesn't need surgery the money can go toward our wedding."

"Glad to hear you haven't forgotten about that." There was laughter in his voice.

"Not likely to forget something like that. I gotta go we're ready to load up. I'll call you tomorrow and let you know when we get there. Doc should have some barn access passes."

"Yeah, Mary and him are both planning to come up with me. I think Mary's just about as excited about you riding as you are."

"That's awesome! I can't wait to see all of you. Bye, sweetie. Love you."

Chapter Fourteen

Calgary! Michelle bounced on the seat as Rolly drove into the barn area and stopped by the shedrow where his stalls were located. The place was crawling with other drivers coming and going. Horses whinnied and kicked at their stalls. The rattle and clang of buckets and other gear made a merry undernote to the cacophony of kids running around playing, horses stamping and people shouting to each other.

It wasn't raining at the moment but the ground was still wet from the overnight storm and the clouds hugged the earth hiding the tall buildings of the downtown core. She jumped down and set about readying the stalls. Piling a deep bed of straw into each stall, she distributed water and feed buckets before putting flakes of hay into hay nets and hanging them safely in each horse's stall. Clay and Hal showed up along with Rolly's mom and dad. Sharon, his long suffering girlfriend poked her head in the door as Michelle fastened the hay net in the last stall.

"Hey, Michelle. That man of mine got you working like a slave?"

"Hi Sharon! You get that RV parked in a good spot? How was the drive down?" Michelle stepped out of the stall and hugged her.

"It was okay. Had to stop by the office. It's has been busy while I was up at Ponoka. But, with the drop in oil though things are really starting to slow down. Things aren't looking good for the oil patch."

"That sucks. When the oil stops so does everything else." Michelle frowned.

Rolly grabbed Sharon around the waist from behind and swung her off her feet. She squealed in surprise and kissed him soundly when he set her on her feet.

"Get a room," Clay heckled them as he walked by pushing the cart loaded with hay bales toward the feed stall.

"You guys got this under control? I'm taking my girl somewhere we can have a little privacy," Rolly announced. He kept his arm firmly around Sharon's waist.

"Sure, go on, get out of here." Hal shooed the couple on their way.

With the efficiency of long practice the horses were soon settled in their stalls and the equipment stowed. Clay and Hal disappeared to renew old acquaintances they hadn't seen for a while. Michelle was at loose ends after they'd gone. She double checked things were in order and then wandered down to visit with some of the other outfits families. One of the Harder girls suggested taking a look at the midway and seeing if the concessions were open yet.

Thursday night before Stampede officially opened with the Friday morning parade, the grounds were opened for Sneak-A-Peek. If they hurried they could get a good look before the public crowded in. The group of them cut across the barns and out the tunnel that ran under the track. Michelle joined in their high-spirited fun, joking about this year's new midway food options. Deep fried chocolate covered pickles, deep fried Mars bars, deep fried bacon wrapped around anything you could think of on a stick, peanut butter and jelly kabobs. Michelle stopped and gapped at the sign proclaiming *Dragon Dog, you gotta try it. $100.00.*

"Are they kidding? *A hundred bucks for a hot dog?*" Michelle shook her head. "I seriously can't believe anyone would pay that."

"Somebody will," Karen Harder assured her. "Some of those big corporate guys trying to impress their buddies."

"I suppose." Michelle was still sceptical.

"Look, a cactus burger. I wanna try one of those." Eva Braithwaite pointed at a food booth further down the fast food alley.

"Jalapeno poutine mini donut bowl?" Sara was incredulous. "Gross, there are some things you just shouldn't mess with. Like mini donuts."

"Too true," Michelle agreed.

When the stands opened and people started filtering in through the gates the girls ate their fill. Michelle wandered back to the barns with a candy apple in jacket pocket holding a cone of candy floss. She pulled bits of it off as she walked. The stuff was pure sugar but it just wasn't Stampede without candy apples, candy floss and sno-cones. The group split up, most of the younger kids headed to the rides on the midway. Michelle continued on the barns with the rest of the group which consisted mostly of wives and the kids too young to running around on their own.

Cale was on call so she wouldn't see him until Monday at the earliest. She contented herself with calling him. It was good to hear his voice and know he was so close. Spud was doing well, but it looked like the surgery might be necessary after all. Doc was behaving more or less and couldn't wait to get to Calgary and hob knob with his cronies at the barns. Mary was threatening to hog tie him if he insisted on crawling all over the chutes during the afternoon performance. The older couple might try to make it up for the Sunday rodeo and chucks, according to Cale Mary was attempting to plan a romantic getaway. She'd booked a room at the Palliser Hotel without telling her husband.

"Just because there's snow on the roof doesn't mean there's no fire in the furnace," Michelle joked trotting out one of Grampa's favorite sayings. She giggled remembering him chasing Gramma around the kitchen table.

"Too much information, Chelly." Cale laughed too.

The long prairie twilight was darkening into true night. Lights shone warmly along the barns and laughter and conversation sounded softly in the dark. The grandstand was dark and empty, the crew was working on setting up the big stage and assembling the wings and other props for the Grandstand Show that ran every night after the wagon races. Behind the bulk of the buildings the lights of the midway shone garishly. The sky was still cloudy but the tall buildings in the downtown glittered faintly in comparison to the neon closer to hand. Red and white lights illuminated the Calgary Tower on Ninth Avenue.

Rolly and the boys were nowhere in sight when she reached the barn. After filling the water buckets and spending a few minutes with each of the horses checking they were comfortable and set for the night, Michelle wended her way toward the RV campground by the Elbow River behind the Saddledome. She passed Rolly's rig without pausing. If she knew the little cowboy as well as she thought she did Karen and him wouldn't appreciate her company. She continued on to the RV Clay and Hal shared. There was an extra bunk she could use anytime she wanted. Cale would be happier knowing she wasn't bedded down in the barn.

A group was gathered around a fire pit by the rig next door. They called for her to join them which she did. It was nice to be part of the familiar comradery of the wagon community. The sport had a long tradition with deep roots. Most of the drivers were related in some way or another, either by marriage or family ties. She settled back with a beer in hand and let the laughter and good natured ribbing wash over her.

* * *

The first two nights of the show went well. The weather held and the track was fast. Rolly's horses ran well and he was just out of the top eight coming into the fourth night of racing. The jitters Michelle had fought with the first few nights were easing off as she gained confidence. Rob was competing in the bull riding and she ran into Kayla back at the barns. The woman looked lost and out of place.

"Hey, Kayla," she greeted her.

"Michelle! Am I ever glad to see you." The woman seized her arm.

"What's wrong?" Apprehension twisted her stomach. "Are you okay? Did Rob have a wreck?" She hadn't heard of anything horrendous happening during the rodeo.

"No, no. I'm fine. Rob's fine. This is just all so strange and I don't know a soul. I'm just glad to see someone I know." She released Michelle's arm.

"Good. You had me scared for a minute. C'mon down to the barn, I have to see to the horses."

Kayla followed her into the barn and perched on a bale in the aisle while Michelle looked after the chores.

"So, what's up?" Michelle sat on a bale beside Kayla's. "Are you enjoying the rodeo so far?"

"I guess. It scares me half to death every time he gets on one of those animals. He just laughs and pats me on the head. Tells me not to worry, he knows what he's doing."

"Well, they're all insane, you know. You'd have to be to keep getting on a bull show after show. But, to give the devil his due, Rob is good at it and does have a pretty good track record of not getting hurt."

"Maybe, but that doesn't help how I feel. I throw up every time he rides," Kayla confessed.

"Does he know that?" Michelle frowned.

"Not a chance. And you can't tell him," she said desperately.

"Why ever not? If it bothers you that much you should at least tell him. Why do you watch him if you hate it so much?"

"I can't tell him. He'll think I'm a baby. Every time I mention something that even hints at how much it upsets me, he goes on and on about how great you were, and how you were always in the stands cheering him on. I have to watch when he rides, it's worse not knowing. But even the thought of it makes me want to be sick."

"I'm sorry, Kayla. Rob has no business throwing me up in your face. He's such a dink. Really, though. You need to sit him down and make him listen to you. Maybe after you've been around the rodeo for a while you'll get

232

used to it? But if it's making you physically sick, that's just not right."

"Thanks, Michelle. Talking to you has helped. I feel better about things now." Kayla got up. "What about you? Aren't you worried about getting hurt charging around the track with all those wagons and other horses?" She looked down at her.

"You don't have time to be afraid. It's the biggest rush you could ever imagine, the speed and the thrill, the danger gives it an edge. I've never felt anything like it."

"Well, I'll be cheering you on tonight from the bleachers. Rob is supposed to meet me, but I've been wandering around for hours and I can't find him."

Michelle got up as well. "Have you tried his cell?"

"He's not answering. It's so frustrating when he does that I could just kill him." She ground her teeth.

"Typical." Michelle snorted. "You can hang around here if you like. Just keep out of the way once the wagons start to roll."

"Thanks. If there's anything I can do to help just let me know."

"Michelle Wilson?" A reporter in shiny boots and a brand spanking new straw hat paused in the door of the barn. Her camera man with the large TV camera perched on his shoulder followed her.

Michelle glanced at Kayla and frowned. "Yeah?" she answered the query. "Can I help you? Are you looking for Rolly?"

"Oh, good. We've found you. No, it's you I want to talk to." The woman advanced into the barn. "This is great, Terry. Just set up here with the horses in the back ground. Michelle if you'd just sit on one of the bales?"

"Okay?" She sat and threw Kayla a bewildered look.

"No, I don't like that. The lighting isn't good. Let's go outside." She set off down the aisle, the camera man trailing behind. "Come on please, Michelle."

"Why do you want to talk to me?" she followed the reporter more out of curiosity than anything else.

"We want to do a spotlight interview with you as one of very few women who have competed as outriders in the wagon racing."

"What?" Michelle was flabbergasted. "I don't think so, really. I don't want to do this."

"Please? Billy Melville was supposed to hunt you up and do the interview but he's still up in the broadcast booth with Tommy. They want to run the spot before or during the evening races."

"Oh, go ahead, Michelle. It'll be fun," Kayla urged her.

"I suppose…"

Her indecision was all encouragement the reporter needed. Before she knew it, the woman had a microphone in Michelle's face and the

234

camera lights were shining in her eyes. Somehow she managed to come up with intelligent responses to the questions and not come off sounding like an idiot. Kayla grinned and cheered her on from behind the camera man. The reporter wrapped up the interview and the camera lights went out.

Michelle blinked for a moment. Kayla hugged her. "You did great! I can't wait to see it later."

"This is Kayla Chetwynd," she said to the reporter who was clearly expecting an introduction to the model pretty woman.

"Chetwynd?" The reporter's ears perked up like a hound picking up a scent. "Are you related to Rob Chetwynd?"

"He's my husband," Kayla replied.

"Husband?" The woman was clearly confused. She glanced at Michelle before going on. "But I thought he was engaged to..." She trailed off, the red of embarrassment staining her cheeks under the TV make up.

"He was," Michelle rescued her. "We split and he married Kayla here."

"Would you be willing to do a spot for us? What it's like being married to a champion bull rider. How do you feel watching him climb on those rank bulls?" The reporter took Kayla by the arm and towed her over in front of Rolly's wagon. The camera lights came to life and before Kayla could protest the woman had launched into her spiel.

Michelle watched in amusement. With any luck they'd run the spot with Kayla and not her. She had to admit the woman was drop dead gorgeous. She'd look good in a feed sack tied with binder twine.

Finally, the TV crew left and the group of kids who had gathered to watch swarmed around Kayla. Entranced by the fact she was not only beautiful but also married to Rob Chetwynd.

Rolly and Karen strolled into view between the barns. Shortly after, Clay and Hal turned up. True to her word, Kayla stayed out of the way. The roar of the crowd and Les McIntyre's distinctive voice let her follow the outcome of the first heats. The clouds gathered in the west and the sky darkened while they harnessed the team Rolly had decided to hook. Michelle glanced at the sky and said a silent prayer the rain would hold off until after their heat.

The big grey was her mount for the night. Hopefully the jackass would stand still and not try to trample her tonight. He was unpredictable but he could run like crazy. Once she was on his back all she had to do was find him room to run and let him go. He knew his job, he was just a handful at the start.

Rolly put his boot on the wheel hub and vaulted into the driver seat. Clay jumped up with him and took the reins for the first pass in front of the grandstand. Michelle waved at Kayla and vaulted onto the grey gelding. He popped his front end, protesting the tight rein,

236

and bounced under her. It was a relief to let him move out a bit as they hit the track. The noise and the commotion of the four wagons taking their practice turns blurred around her. Her nerves were strung tight as the adrenaline surged through her. The gelding picked up on it and fought for his head. Michelle curbed him and jumped down, taking her place behind the wagon with the barrel in her hand. She was trembling so hard she could hardly breathe. Like the horse, she just wanted to run. The gelding bumped into her and his breath was hot on the back of her neck. Hal wrestled the lead team to a standstill and they waited.

The horn went and she lost all coherent thought as she hurled the barrel into the wagon bed. She registered Hal letting the leaders go and leaping onto his horse. The grey lunged and reared, but she was already half on and scrambled the rest of the way without losing any momentum. The barrels flashed by, she allowed herself a moment of satisfaction that they were all still standing. The number two barrel was squashed as she raced by. Bad luck for Chad. The track was open in front of them and the grey lengthened his stride. Around her the press of outrider horses spurred her horse to put on a burst of speed.

Rolly was running on the rail with two wagons three wide beside him. Hal's chestnut came even with her and gave her a wild grin. She smiled back, spitting dirt out of her mouth. They flew around the first turn and into the back stretch. Hard rain suddenly pelted down stinging her face. The grey gelding squealed as the rain turned to hail. She hid her face in his mane and pulled a set of goggles down over her eyes. The fourth wagon was on the rail a few lengths in front and on the rail. The driver seemed to be trying to pull them up but the wall of rain and hail made it hard to tell.

The crack of splitting wood was louder than the storm. Michelle straightened up and pulled hard on the gelding's mouth. The wagon jack knifed wildly and she screamed at the horse to listen to her and pull up a bit. She needed to steer him more to the outside away from the possibility of a wreck. The gelding finally changed course and she breathed a sigh of relief. It turned to a gasp of horror as the wagon lurched off the rail and Carl was pitched out. He landed over the rail in the infield near as she could tell. There was no body under the churning hooves or the wagon wheels.

One of his outriders pulled behind and made a dive for the back of the wagon. He missed and slid in the mud as she flashed by. She prayed the other riders would be able to miss him. The grey snatched the bit in his teeth and increased his speed again. The driverless horses were running wild and the wagon slewed behind them. *The tongue snapped.* They were almost to the top of the lane. She glanced around, no one was closer to the leaders than her. Without consciously making a decision, she urged the gelding up beside the wagon. The horses thundered along doing what they were bred to do. The spinning hub was close to the grey's legs. Michelle didn't dare ask him to move over anymore. The hoop holding the tarp was tantalizingly close to her hand. If she just reached out, grabbed it and jumped... Inexplicably the grey moved closer to the wagon and Michelle jumped. She hit the seat, half on and half off. Scrambling to her knees she searched for the flying tangle of lines. Not bothering to try and sort the wet leather she wrapped them around her hands, braced her feet against the front of the wagon and hauled for all she was worth. They pounded around the last turn, she lungs burned with the effort and she pulled on the horses harder. Without warning another pair of hands took hold of the reins as well. Together they managed to slow the team to a barely controlled canter. As they crossed in front of the grandstand more outriders caught the leaders and brought them under control.

Michelle collapsed onto her knees trembling too hard to even pull herself up onto the seat. She glanced at the man behind her. Arlo grinned back at her. He unwrapped the lines from her wrists and climbed over the back of the seat. They continued toward the barns without stopping. A disassociated part of her brain registered that the horses all seemed to fine, no uneven gait that she could see in any of them. She spared a thought for the grey gelding, if he hadn't swerved toward the wagon as she jumped...Better not to think about that.

The wagon rattled off the track and stopped by the barns. She tried to get up but her right arm wouldn't work properly. Stupidly, she stared at it lying on her thigh. It looked swollen, and all black and red. People were talking to her but it didn't really register in her brain for a moment.

"No, I'm fine. I'm fine." Michelle shoved herself upright and went to jump down. Arms caught her as she slid, keeping her from face planting. "I'm fine," she repeated. "How's Carl? Is he okay? And the guy who missed the wagon?"

"They took them to the hospital as a precaution but they should be good as new," Cale's voice spoke by her ear.

"Cale?"

"Yeah, I'm here. Mary and Doc too."

"Michelle Wilson! What in the name of all that's holy did you think you were doing out there?" Mary scolded her while crying at the same time.

"You did good, girl," Doc's voice was gruff.

Her knees threatened to fold under her. At least the damn storm had passed.

"You need to see a doctor," Cale insisted.

"Michelle, are you okay?" Rolly appeared in her line of vision. "What you did was crazy."

"Where's Grey? Is he okay? He didn't get hurt did he?" She looked up. "I'm sorry I cost you two seconds."

"For Christ sake, Michelle. You and Arlo saved a wreck. Don't apologize." Rolly raked his hand through his wet hair.

Red and blue lights reflected off the barns. Cale coaxed her toward the EMS who hurried toward them. The pain in her wrist threatened to make her puke. She supported her wrist with the other hand but nothing she did made it comfortable. The other wrist was throbbing as well, but at least it still obeyed her.

Everything blurred around her. The next thing she was aware of, the ambulance was bouncing out of the grounds and Cale was sitting beside her hanging onto a strap.

"Hey. Where are we going? I'm fine." She tried to sit up. The EMS by her head pressed her back with a hand on her shoulder.

"Lie still, Michelle. It looks like you might have broken your wrist. It was all tangled up in the reins. Cale rested a hand on her leg. "Both your hands are pretty beat up and you've got bruises all over your face from the hail."

"What the hell was that anyway? Freaking hail storm in the middle of the race. What shitty timing." She was annoyed her words slurred. They must have put something in the IV she didn't remember them starting in her arm. It itched and she wanted to rip it out, but it was in her good arm and the other one was immobilized.

The vehicle lurched and came to a stop. The doors opened and she closed her eyes against the glare of the lights. The EMS unloaded the

241

stretcher as gently as they could but the jarring brought tears to her eyes. Now the shock was wearing off a bit, not only her arm hurt, but her hands and shoulder throbbed. One hip sent sharp shooting pains down her leg and up her back.

"Shit, shit, shit," she muttered. They wheeled her through the sliding doors into the ER. She twisted her head. "Cale? Cale?"

"Shush, honey. The doctors have to look at you, then they'll let your friend in to see you," the attendant at her head said.

To her annoyance tears burned her eyes and ran down her face. *Great, now I'm blubbering like a baby.* She sniffed and struggled to gain control of her emotions. When she was able to pay attention to what was going on around her again, the EMS had handed her over to the hospital staff. She was whisked into a curtained cubicle and blond doctor hustled in. He asked some questions and she must have answered them because he wrote things down on his clipboard. The overhead lights shone on his blond hair and she thought about how pretty he was standing there all officious like. She must have dozed off because the next thing she knew he was gone and she didn't remember him leaving. *Huh, good drugs.* She giggled.

"Good to hear you laughing." Cale came through the opening in the curtains.

"When can I get out of here?" She struggled to sit up and stopped when her vision blurred. "Damn."

"I talked to the doctor. They want to do x-rays on your arms and hands. Maybe your hip." Cale leaned over and kissed her gently on the forehead.

"My hip?" She shifted and grimaced.

"You told the doctor your hip was hurting." Cale told her.

"Me and my big mouth. Must be the stupid drugs." Her lips twisted in an attempt to smile.

"How much do you remember?" Cale asked her.

"I remember the wagon tongue breaking and it was hailing. It hurt. Then the next thing I remember was being in the wagon and trying to get a grip on the wet reins. I think I wrapped them around my hands. Somehow, Arlo got there…Then not much til we got back to the barns. Oh! Carl, how's Carl. He got thrown out of the wagon didn't he?" She turned her head away. "I think I'm gonna puke," she managed to say.

Cale held the bowl while she heaved. "Fuck, that hurt." Michelle lay back on the pillow sweating and exhausted. "What about Carl?"

"He's shook up. I think maybe he broke a collarbone or something. He was in the ER but I'm not sure if he's still here or not." Cale smoothed the hair back from her forehead.

She closed her eyes for a moment. Loud voices and a commotion outside the curtain roused her.

"I don't care what your rules are. You tell me where she is," Mary was in full cry threatening anyone who stood between her and Michelle with a slow and painful death.

"Now, Mary." That was Doc playing peace maker. She smiled at Cale who ducked out through the curtain.

Seconds later Mary burst into the cubicle. "Michelle Wilson, have you no sense? You could have been killed." She stopped to draw breath.

"Leave her be, Mary. Her and Arlo probably saved some lives tonight. I'm proud of you, girl." Doc beamed down at her, his eyes shiny with tears.

"I didn't do anything anyone else wouldn't have done in the same position," she protested.

"Maybe some would, maybe some wouldn't," Doc said.

"I was scared the horses were gonna get hurt. I knew Grey would take care of himself. He is okay isn't he? I don't remember seeing him afterward." Her heart squeezed in her chest. If he was hurt it was her fault and she couldn't live with that.

"He's bright eyed and bushy tailed, that boy. Came strutting back to the barn proud as peacock, like he was king shit," Doc told her.

"Thank God for that. I still feel guilty about Spud, if I hurt Grey too…I don't know what I'd do." She closed her eyes for a second to hide the tears that threatened.

Doc took Mary's arm. "We should go. You've seen with your own eyes Michelle is doing okay. I want to find out if Carl is still here. I don't know if they let him go or if he got admitted."

Mary kissed Michelle and gently squeezed her least damaged hand. "If you need anything you call me, hear? You take care of her," she said the last to Cale as Doc herded his wife out through the curtain.

Cale had just settled in the chair by the bed when a porter arrived to take her to x-ray. It was late when another porter brought her back. Cale was asleep leaning back in the uncomfortable chair. "Hey." He yawned. "You feeling any better?"

"I think so. It still hurts but it doesn't make me want to hurl anymore."

A different doctor came in. "Hello, Michelle. I hear you're quite the hero. You rodeo people are keeping us busy today." He continued without waiting for a response. "I've looked at your x-rays. Your right arm is badly bruised but I can't see any fractures. Everything seems to be aligned. We might need to recheck it once the swelling goes down a bit. Your left arm however, is broken between the wrist and the elbow. Both the radius and the ulna are involved. We're going to reduce the fracture and put in a couple of plates and screws to stabilize it. This type of injury often results in a condition called compartment syndrome. The swelling restricts the blood flow to the hand and lower

245

arm. It's extremely painful and can result in loss of sensation and function. It typically occurs within 24 to 48 hours of the injury or surgery. If you experience any of those sensations let someone know immediately."

"I don't want surgery," Michelle protested when he finally let her get a word in.

"It's not an option I'm afraid. We can't treat it conservatively because of the amount of displacement of the bones." He carefully uncovered the injured arm and pointed to a place where the skin was already purple and discoloured. One place stuck up quite sharply. Looking at it threatened to make her hurl again. Michelle swallowed hard. "As you can see, that's an end of bone poking up. It hasn't broken the skin at this point but the bone is extremely sharp and there's the risk it become a compound fracture or injure nearby nerves or blood vessels."

"Don't argue, Chelly. Just let the doctor do his job." Cale's voice sounded choked.

"If you'll just sign the consent form," the surgeon said after he explained the risks of the surgery to her. He held the clipboard for her while she scrawled her name on the line. "It won't be too much longer. I'll put an order in for more pain meds to keep you comfortable."

"Thanks, doctor," Cale said before the man whisked out through the curtains.

A nurse showed up a few minutes later and injected something into the IV. "That's morphine and some Gravol. Some people experience nausea from the morphine." She smiled and left.

"Close your eyes and try to rest, sweetie." Cale kissed her forehead and pushed her hair behind her ear. "You really need to quit making a habit of ending up in the hospital."

"I know." She chuckled weakly. "Don't leave, okay?"

"I'll always be here, come hell or high water. Love you." His voice faded although his lips were still moving.

Michelle tried to tell him something but the words wouldn't come. The world blurred and she drifted off into a dream where horses were running around her and she couldn't catch them. Somewhere a crowd was roaring and wagons were rolling, but she couldn't see them.

Chapter Fifteen

Rhythmic pounding dragged Michelle into consciousness. She rolled over, forgetting about her injured arm. The sharp pain brought her fully awake. Rubbing sleep from her eyes with her less wounded hand, she blinked and focused on the grey light coming through the bedroom window.

Water sheeted down the pane, outside the prairie grasses whipped in the wind. She wriggled up on the pillows til she was more upright. *Is it ever going to stop raining?* In the two weeks since the surgery the weather had been wet off and on, but four days ago a front stalled against the Rockies and heavy rain pounded the southern Alberta prairies.

Michelle eased the bandaged arm on the blanket trying to find a more comfortable spot. Earlier, when Cale unwrapped the tensor wrap and exposed the site, the skin was still swollen from above her elbow all the down into her hand and fingers. She attempted to wriggle her fingers now and gritted her teeth in frustration when the only movement was a tiny twitch. The surgeon assured her before leaving the hospital that the function should return once the swelling subsided. The metallic line of staples marching down her forearm made her slightly nauseous, it was like looking at someone else's arm, not her own. Cale said that was a normal reaction, but it was seriously weird in her opinion.

"Cale?" Her voice echoed in the hall outside the open bedroom door. Storm raised her head and thumped her tail on the floor beside the bed. Crazy Puppy came skidding through the door and bounced up on the bottom of the bed. "Get down, you ass." Michelle kicked at him with her foot. "Down. Now." The young dog woofed, tongue lolling out of his grinning mouth. He ignored her commands, turned once and flopped down in a heap. "Cale!" She tried again.

No one answered. Cale must have gone into the clinic or got called out. He'd stuck pretty close to home so far, but Carrie and Doc couldn't carry the load forever. She picked up the phone from the bedside table and then replaced it. There was no reason she couldn't be on her own for a while. It wasn't like she was a baby or something. A blast of wind rattled the window along with a fresh flood or rain. Michelle pulled the covers up over her shoulder, sliding the injured arm into the welcome warmth.

The alarm on the clock radio beeped loudly. "Oh, shut up!" She managed to silence the noise. Reaching for the plastic container beside her, she got it open and shook out a pain pill. Sticking it into her mouth she picked up the water glass Cale had thoughtfully left filled with ice. Most of the cubes were melted, the cold fluid helped chase the dryness from her mouth.

Michelle had tried skipping some meds. She hated taking pills and being dependent on drugs, but the pain convinced her otherwise. "I've turned into a wuss," she told Storm who rested her head on the edge of the bed. The damn things might help with the throbbing but they made her stupid and sleepy. *All I do is sleep anymore.* A yawn cracked her jaw. Irritated she turned her head on the pillow and glared at the rain soaked corrals. Refusing to give in to the urge to nap, Michelle rummaged in the blankets for the TV remote. The noon news was on, the weather man looked suitably serious as he discussed the persistent weather front.

Pictures of swollen streams and flooded low lying areas zipped across the screen. She forced herself to concentrate at the sight of the Bow River flooding the zoo in downtown Calgary. "Holy man!" A huge tree beside a flooded bike path shuddered and toppled into the raging river. "I didn't think it was that bad." The station shifted to a report from a woman standing in Mission, a Calgary suburb close to the river. She stood at the edge of a river of water covering the street and inundating lawns and houses. The fire hydrant behind her was submerged more than half way up its length. The reporter pointed at it and told the audience how rapidly the water was rising, using the hydrant as a flood gauge.

Michelle dialed Mary and waited impatiently for her to pick up. "Mary, have you seen the news?"

"I know. How horrible. I just talked to Nora in High River. She's packing up whatever she can, they're under evacuation notice."

"Oh my God. What can we do to help?"

"*You* can do nothing, missy. Just stay put," Mary was adamant. "We've offered to go and pick up any stock that's in danger. A lot of people on high ground have offered to take them in."

"What about the dogs and cats and stuff," Michelle worried.

"The local rescues and humane societies are putting up what they can. I just can't believe how much rain is falling."

"I know. How high is the Highwood? It must be in danger of flooding too. Damn, there's stock in the lower pasture." She kicked back the covers and the puppy landed on the floor with a thump.

"Michelle! Stop, right now. Cale and Doc brought them up late last night when the river started to really rise. You stay put or so help me I'll come out there and hog tie you."

She subsided back onto the pillows. "Are you sure? The cattle are safe and on high ground?"

"Don't you trust Doc? And Cale? I've never lied to you?"

"I know. I just feel so damned helpless lying here like a beached whale," she

251

complained. "I should be out helping with sandbags, or at least I could drive the truck and trailer and go transport animals."

"Quit talking nonsense. You'd be putting yourself in danger not to mention those you're trying to help. It's only been two weeks since you got hurt, don't be stupid."

The television showed the Deerfoot in Calgary by Anderson Road, the Bow River raged across it, swollen and carrying broken trees and debris with it. "Oh my God! Mary do you see what's on the news right now? The river's over the Deerfoot!"

"Oh my stars! I can't believe this is happening. It's all coming downstream. Okotoks, High River and the reserves are going to get hit badly. Look Michelle, I'm gonna let you go. I need to call some people and start making plans for evacuees and their animals. The community centres on high ground can house a lot of them, but it's gonna take a lot of work to get it set up. And we need to figure out how to feed them all. You stay put, you hear me?"

"Let me know if I can do something. At least I can make calls." Michelle frowned at the phone as the line went dead. She dialed Cale, but it went straight to voice mail. "Looks like we're on our own, dogs." She sat up and put her feet on the floor. Her head swam a bit and she waited for the vertigo to subside. "Damn pain meds." Cale thoughtfully left a walking stick leaning by the bed. She took it in her good hand

and carefully stood up. "So far so good." Storm looked up at her, Crazy Puppy opened an eye and then went back to sleep on the foot of the bed. "Great, now I'm talking to myself."

Maneuvering carefully she moved toward the door using the bed for support. She paused as the end of it and waited for the intense throbbing in her arm to ease a bit. The short distance to the door took forever to negotiate. Leaning on the wall for support she finally reached the kitchen. Cale had left a thermos of tea on the table and a sandwich.

Grinning in triumph she made it to the table and sank into a chair. Opening the thermos with one hand was a bit of a challenge. The hot liquid warmed her from the inside out. Michelle felt much better after eating the sandwich. The phone on the desk shrilled in the silent house. She got up and reached it before it quit ringing.

"Michelle, it's Stacey," she sounded panicked. "I hate to bother you. I know you're still recovering…"

"Quit the drama, what is it? What's wrong?" Michelle cut her off.

"I just fed the cows and counted heads. There's two cow-calf pairs missing. They're in the coulee. I can see them and the river's getting close to where they are."

"Damn!" Michelle made her way to the window overlooking the coulee between Cale's and her childhood home. Huddled against the side of the coulee at the bottom, tails turned to the driving rain, the cattle were barely visible.

The angry mass of muddy water loaded with huge trees and unfortunate dead animals swirling in the turbulent current was only a few feet away from them. "Stacey, listen to me. You have to leave them. There's no way to reach them in time."

"I can't. I keep seeing those big brown calf eyes and I just can't stand it. Which horse do you think can make it down there and back? I don't know who to saddle."

"Stacey, no!"

"Michelle, I have to. I can't just let them drown without trying," she wailed. "Are you going to help me or not?"

"Be reasonable. What do you want me to do?" Michelle snapped.

"Look, I realize you're not in any shape to actually come and help me. But tell me which horse to take, what should I take with me? How do I get the cows to follow me?"

"Stacey, you can't. Do you hear me? Even if I wasn't hurt I'd think twice before trying something that dangerous," Michelle tried to reason with her. Her head hurt now and her arm was throbbing again.

"Like hell! You'd be down there in a heartbeat and you know it. Look, I don't have time to argue with you. The river's rising." Stacey hung up.

"Oh for fuck's sake." She set the phone down and returned to the table. Her knees gave out and she more fell than sat into the chair. The doctor said she had a mild concussion, but surely it should be better by now. When she quit seeing double, Michelle got to her feet and looked out the window. Leaning on the wide sill for support she squinted into the driving rain. "God damn it!" Barely visible, a horse and rider stood at the top of the trail down into the coulee. The rider's red jacket was what caught her eye. That and the blonde hair streaming in the wind. "Don't do it. Don't do it." The pair started down the steep slope.

Michelle hesitated for a minute. Then she returned to the desk as fast as her legs would take her. She picked up the phone and hit the speed dial. "Mary, thank God you answered. Listen. Can you get a hold of Doc or Cale, or anybody? Stacey's headed down to the river to try and rescue some cows. I couldn't talk her out of it."

"What are you talking about?" Mary demanded. "I'm not sure where the men are right now."

"Stacey is on her way down the west trail into the coulee. The river's rising fast." She ran out of breath.

"Okay. You stay put. I'll try and reach Luke and Cale. If I can't, I'll find someone to go help. You stay put." Mary reiterated.

Michelle hung up and returned to the window. The bright spot that was Stacey was a quarter of the way down the trail. She held her breath when the horse slid for a bit before regaining its footing. Below, the river had risen higher. The time was running out for the cattle.

Making a decision, Michelle left the cane leaning against the table and went to the mud room. Shrugging into her oilskin, she hissed as the sleeve pressed on the staples under the thick wrapping. It didn't bend well but at least she could get her arm in. Snatching the keys to the farm truck off the hook by the door she battled the wind and reached the truck.

It was oddly still inside after the wailing wind and rain outside. She inserted the key and turned the ignition. A smile of triumph lit her face when the engine came to life. Now was no time for old truck to be cantankerous. The gravel road was rutted with runnels of water flooding over it. The ass end skidded when she turned into the lane under the Wilson Ranch sign. She drove right up to the barn and gingerly stepped down from the vehicle, cradling her arm.

The wind wrestled with her when she opened the barn door. Relief surged over her at the sight of a buckskin head poked over a stall door. "Hey, Toad," she greeted the gelding. "Ready to be like the cavalry and ride to the rescue." He whickered in response. A saddle sat on its nose by the stall with a bridle and pad draped over it. It was slow tacking him up with only one hand but she managed. The horse was reluctant to go out into the storm but followed readily after hesitating in the door.

She hooked the reins over the horn and managed to pull herself up into the saddle. Toad moved off before she was quite settled, the wet reins slipping a bit in her hand. Touching him with her heel she trotted over to the top of the coulee where the trail dipped over the edge. Stacey was about three-quarters of the way down. "Stacey! Hey! Wait for me!" The rider below never hesitated. The rain and wind must drown out her voice. Closing her eyes to ease the pain in her head she waited a moment for it subside a bit. Opening them, she started down the incline. The muddy clay was slick underfoot. The gelding sat on his haunches and slid twenty feet. "Stacey! Wait!"

The red-coated rider glanced back, blonde hair streaming in her face. She lifted a hand and waved but kept moving. Michelle gritted her teeth and navigated the switchback in the trail before taking the next downward section. Stacey reached the bottom and halted. A minute later Toad came up beside her.

"Michelle, thanks for coming," Stacey shouted. "What do we do now?" She waved at the shivering cows and calves huddled in the dubious shelter of some bushes. The roar of the river was louder than the wind down here in the bottom land.

"We need to get behind them and convince them to go up. Just be careful, the ground is soft. We need to hurry and get out of here though." Michelle glanced at the raging torrent a few feet away. "You go first and get them moving. I'll stay here in case they decide to go toward the river. Toad and I can turn them."

The blonde nodded and eased her horse around the cattle. Michelle moved back a few feet to give them a clear path up the trail. "Wave your hat at them," she screamed over the noise.

Stacey hollered and slapped her hat on her wet thigh. The cows raised their heads and bawled but didn't move. The blonde shouted again and tried to swat the nearest one with her long reins. It jumped forward and the calf went with it. Michelle waited, glancing behind her where the river edged closer to the horse's heels.

"Keep at it!" she encouraged. The damn cow doubled back. Gritting her teeth, Michelle moved Toad carefully by them and joined Stacey. "Okay, we're gonna shove them and hope they go up and not into the river. You ready?"

Stacey nodded.

"Follow me. Do what I do, your horse knows what he's doing, let him do his job. If the cows go in the river let the damn things go. Don't go after them." The pain in her arm made her want to puke. The shivers shaking her body weren't helping. "You wave, I can't and steer too." Without waiting for an answer she moved Toad toward the cows. He shoved a shoulder into one and it moved in the direction they wanted. Stacey got the other pair to follow. Michelle held her breath until the first pair set foot on the upward slope. She held back and let the other cow and calf go ahead of her. "Okay, now we just need to keep them moving," she shouted to the other girl. "You go ahead."

Stacey started up after the cows. Toad quivered under her, twitching at the huge pieces of flotsam that rushed past just a few feet away. Once the other horse was far enough ahead, Michelle gave Toad his head. Her stomach clenched and flipped as his hind end dropped out from under her. The bank they were standing on collapsed into the river. The buckskin threw himself forward and clawed back onto semi-solid ground. Between the pain in her head and with the use of only one hand, Michelle slid out of the saddle. The rain blurred her vision and her head spun. There was no way she was going to get back on the horse. Stacey was a quarter of the way up the coulee, obviously unaware Michelle was in danger. Another old cottonwood uprooted by the river bobbed by, its branches scraping along the ragged bank.

Toad nudged her with his nose, eyes showing white around the edges. He wouldn't leave her until she gave him permission. She looped the dragging reins around the horn and swatted him on the ass. "Go on, git!" Tears of frustration mingled with the rain on her face. Toad refused to move, shoving his head into her chest. "Go on!" He rolled his eyes but stood fast. Tearing a switch off a bush she whacked him as hard as she could. "Git! Go, you jackass!" Snorting the gelding surged up the track, mud flying from under his sliding hooves.

Water soaked her jeans and ran down the back of her neck. The river lapped around her ankles, sucking at the earth under her feet. Michelle scrambled up the bank unto the trail. She grabbed at the bushes on the side with her good hand. Falling to her knees she gasped at the pain shooting up her arm. *If the damn hand would just work.* Somehow she regained her footing and inched another few feet away from the river. She looked up, rain running off her hair and down her face. She'd lost her hat somewhere, damn it. Toad's buckskin rump disappeared around the switchback above her. Letting go of the scraggly bush beside her, Michelle lunged for one further up. Her fingers closed on the branch, prickly thorns tearing her palm. *"Fucking thorn bush!"*

By the time she managed to reach the third switchback her legs refused to take her any farther. She glanced down where the river raged and leaned against the steep side of the coulee as it rose above her. The water wouldn't come this high. At least she hoped so. *It doesn't matter, I can't go any farther. I'll just sit here for a minute until I feel a bit better.* Her teeth chattered and her jaw ached from it. The cold must have numbed the pain in her arm because she barely felt it. A fresh gust of wind and rain hit her face. Michelle hunched down in her oilskin and tried to hide her face. Wide rivulets of muddy clay and water rolled down the trail digging deep ruts as it went. She collapsed onto her butt, legs curled in front of her. She pushed ineffectively at the wet mess pooling around her with her good hand. *Cold, so cold. I'd kill for a coffee and Baileys.* The world slipped away from her. The cold faded to be replaced by blissful nothingness. Someone called her name and she resisted leaving the warm safe place she found herself in.

"Michelle!" No, someone was definitely shaking her.

"Toad, go on. Git!" She flapped her good hand. "No sense both of us drowning, jackass."

"Michelle. C'mon, wake up a bit." Hand hooked under her arms and her feet slid beneath her.

"Leave me alone," she muttered refusing to open her eyes.

"Chelly, it's me. C'mon, you've got to help me. Here! I found her." He must have been speaking to someone else.

Found who? More voices intruded on her conscious and another pair of hands held her upright. Finally dragged out of her safe refuge Michelle opened her eyes in irritation.

"Cale?" Rain plastered his dark hair to his head, mud streaked his face and clothes, but it was definitely him. "What are you doing here?

"Chelly? Thank God. Don't worry, we'll get you out of here. Try to help us as much as you can. We'll be as gentle as possible with your arm."

She allowed herself to be hauled up the steep incline with a minimal amount of cussing. Or so she thought. Once on solid ground Mary's face swam into view and she wrapped her in a warm wool blanket.

"Do you ever listen to anything I say?" she scolded.

"Stacey! Where's Stacey and the cows. Did Toad get up okay?" Michelle looked around wildly.

"Hush. They're all fine. Stacey had a hot shower and Mary's got her tucked up in bed with hot water bottles." Cale picked her up and carried her into the familiar kitchen. Gramma's big old wood stove throwing welcome heat from its place in the corner.

"How did you find me?" Her teeth chattered.

"When Toad came up without you Stacey was frantic. She was just about to go back for you when Doc and I showed up with help," Cale explained.

"But why were you here in the first place?" Nothing was making any sense.

"You called Mary, remember? You told her about the cows and Stacey wanting to go after them. She managed to reach me and I called some neighbors, and when we got here Stacey had just come up out of the coulee with the cows. Toad was right behind her, but there was no sign of you."

"The bank collapsed and I fell off. Couldn't get back on. No sense Toad drowning because I'm stupid." Michelle shivered harder.

"Search and Rescue is on its way, but I couldn't wait for them. We went looking for you. God, Michelle. I thought you were in the damned river." He buried his face in her lap.

"I was coming. I just had to wait. I was so tired. I would have made it up eventually," she insisted.

"Like hell." Mary snorted by her side and pressed a hot drink into her good hand.

"You're an idiot," Cale grumbled lifting his head from her lap. "You should have known I'd find you. I told you before…"

"I know, I know. Come hell or high water, you'll always be by my side."

"Come hell or high water," he repeated.

The kitchen door let in a wash of cold air and the scent of mud and rain. "Ambulance is here," Doc announced.

"Don't want an ambulance," Michelle protested.

"Humour me." Cale helped the EMS strip off her wet clothes, get her on the gurney and wrap her in warm blankets. "Between the Half a Mile of Hell, the High Wood River and your stubborn Wilson pride I'm gonna be an old man before my time."

"But I love you," Michelle reminded him as they bumped the gurney down porch steps and into the back of the waiting ambulance.

"I love you, too." Cale climbed into the ambulance behind her for the second time in a month. "Promise me you aren't going to make a habit of this. We've got a date for next May you can't miss."

"Promise," she said as the unit pulled out of the yard.

The End

Other books by this author from Books We Love

Longview Romances

Storm's Refuge
A Longview Christmas

The Cornwall Adventures Series
Laurel's Quest
A Step Beyond
Go Gently

Arabella's Secret Series
The Selkie's Song

Historical Fiction
No Absolution by N.M. Bell

About the Author

Nancy M Bell has publishing credits in poetry, fiction and non-fiction. Nancy has presented at the Surrey International Writers Conference and the Writers Guild of Alberta Conference. She loves writing fiction and poetry and following wherever her muse takes her.

Please visit her webpage
http://www.nancymbell.ca
You can find her on Facebook at
http://facebook.com/NancyMBell
Follow on twitter: @emilypikkasso

Books We Love Ltd.
http://bookswelove.net